ONE PLUS ONE

Maths, Book Two

P.A. Friday

Published by
NineStar Press
PO Box 91792
Albuquerque, New Mexico, 87199
www.ninestarpress.com

Warning: This book contains sexually explicit content, which is only suitable for mature readers.

Print ISBN #978-1-947139-53-4
Cover by Natasha Snow
Edited by BJ Toth

James Cape has been in love with his mother's best friend Laurie since James was sixteen and Laurie an inaccessible twenty-six. When he's turned down flat by the older man just after his nineteenth birthday, James's best friend Al encourages him to forget Laurie and find someone else. And James tries, he really does. But can he cope with his feelings for Laurie, his best friend's home-life problems, and the deteriorating health of his father, all at the same time? And will Laurie ever notice the young man who's right in front of him?

Dedication

To Rosemary and Nikki, with love.

Acknowledgements

Thanks need to go to so many people who helped with editing. Rosemary and BJ in particular, but also the later editors and proofreaders. Thank you so much; it makes a difference and I know it.

Thanks and love also go to my two boys, who cope with living with a writer. James, you are my rock (and many thanks for the plot help!) and Cameron, you are the best and I hope you know it.

Chapter One

JAMES CAPE WAS fourteen years old when he realised he was gay, fifteen when he came out to his best friend, and sixteen when he realised how he'd recognised he was gay in the first place. He'd thought he'd 'just known' until his mother's friend Laurie came over one day with his new boyfriend, Kieran—the first boyfriend he'd ever bothered bringing round—and James had felt his heart explode with jealousy and rage. Kieran couldn't have Laurie. Laurie belonged with him.

The longed-for relationship wasn't—quite—as inappropriate as it might have sounded. Laurie was his mother's friend, yes, but he wasn't his mother's age. Gillie, James's mum, was thirty-nine; Laurie, twenty-six. They'd met online when James was about nine and had made friends over the next year, despite the age gap. When Gillie had discovered that Laurie was a student at the university she herself taught at, she'd invited him over, and he'd become a regular visitor. To start with, James hadn't been much interested—the gap between ten years old and twenty was a big one, and James had been more interested in playing with Al, his best friend both then and now. Between them, the pair had teased and hassled and joked around with Laurie, treating him as something between a friend and an older brother; but as the years had passed, James's feelings towards Laurie had changed. He just hadn't realised quite how much they had changed until Laurie turned up with Kieran by his side.

It wasn't as if Laurie had never had boyfriends in the past. He had. But he'd never brought them over to James's house before, and that made all the difference. When Laurie had been at James's house, he hadn't belonged to anyone else. He'd been theirs. With Kieran there, the dynamic was different—spoilt. Al, also over for the weekend—as usual—cocked a knowing eyebrow at James's moodiness and dragged him out for a long walk.

"You don't like the boyfriend," Al said when they were in the woods and miles from anywhere. Trust Al to get straight to the point.

James shrugged. "Bit of a wanker, that's all. Laurie could do better."

"Mm." Al didn't sound convinced. "D'you remember telling me that you weren't interested in Laura Fielding because Mary MacDonald had bigger tits?"

"What?" James looked at his best mate in bewilderment. "That was nearly two years ago. Why are you bringing that up again?"

"You weren't interested in Laura Fielding because she was a girl, and you weren't interested in girls," Al said bluntly. "By the way, I'm still pissed off it took you nearly a year to tell me you were gay. You can't have thought I'd give a toss."

"You're still the only person who knows," James pointed out.

James and Al's school was not the sort of place where it was safe to be 'out'. James had no intention of telling anyone else about his sexuality until he'd left. Telling Al was different—Al was Al. And he was quite right; James knew he could tell Al anything and Al wouldn't care. You could say what you liked about Al—and most people did—but he was intensely loyal. To James, at any rate. When it came to relationships, it was a different matter. Unlike James, Al liked girls and had a steady stream of girlfriends, but none of them lasted longer than a month before he got itchy. Usually it was considerably shorter.

"They get so clingy," Al had complained. "They want stuff."

"That's called dating," James had told him unsympathetically.

He was amazed anyone still agreed to go out with Al, but there was something about his best friend. He had a strange sort of manic charm, and his very unpredictability seemed to draw people in. However, that was a different matter. Why Al had gone back to harping about old news, James couldn't imagine.

"Thing is," Al said, scuffing the last of the autumn leaves with his shoe—the woods didn't seem to have cottoned on to the fact that it was March, "it didn't have anything to do with Mary MacDonald."

"Al, you've lost me."

Al—so very like James to look at in some ways: dark-haired, regular features, similar body shape, albeit several inches shorter—looked seriously at his friend.

"It's not Kieran you don't like," he said. "It's Laurie having a boyfriend."

"He's had boyfriends before," James said defensively.

"Ah. Hasn't brought them home, though, has he? Different thing altogether."

James shrugged petulantly. "I just think Kieran's an idiot, that's all."

Al knew when to stop—usually. "Whatever you say, mate. Just...don't piss Laurie off by being too rude to his guy, you know? Probably a bad plan."

Which, as James admitted and worked by, was a sensible idea. But when Laurie turned up a fortnight later alone, James couldn't help his heart lifting.

"No Kieran?" he asked, hoping Laurie would say that they'd broken up.

Laurie gave him a lazy smile. "No, not this time. I wanted you lot to myself. Any objections?"

"Nope."

The weather was nice, and they were all sitting out in the garden, drinking beer. James and Al—who spent considerably more weekends at James's house than at his own, to the point that Gillie and Terry, James's dad, had assigned the spare bedroom as belonging to him—had been told that one was their limit, to Al's laughing protest. James had his guitar out and was strumming it from time to time. He had a passion for music and already knew that he wanted to study it at university; it was just a case of getting through GCSEs (now only a few months away) and A levels first. Al was more interested in drama and films, which gave him something in common with Laurie, who was currently working on a PhD in Film Studies, focusing on bringing books to life as films, with particular emphasis on the *Lord of the Rings* trilogy. The trilogy was special in another way—Gillie and Laurie had met via an online discussion board about the films and had found they got on well, moving from there to talking about everything under the sun. "And some things not under it," Gillie usually added at this point, as science fiction and astrophysics had also been discussed. James joked that his mum was a science geek on the quiet.

"Just surprised you could bear to be parted from him," Al added cheekily.

Laurie took a gulp of beer and shook his head sadly at Al. "We're twenty-six, not sixteen, Al. We can manage to be parted for an entire afternoon without dying of angst. You might be like that, but we're not."

James snorted. "Al? Seriously? God knows why he has girlfriends because he seems to spend all his time hiding from them once he's dating them."

"An interesting approach."

"I like snogging them and suchlike," Al said cheerfully. "It's just the rest of it which is a bother. Is it like that with you, Laurie, then? You've only got your bloke for the snogging? And the suchlike," he added thoughtfully.

James tried not to blush at the thought of Laurie doing 'the suchlike' with Kieran. It seemed Laurie was having a similar problem as he choked back a laugh.

"I can't say I object to that side of things, but no, there's a little more to it than that, thanks."

"Al, are you teasing Laurie again?" Gillie called from where she was chatting animatedly with James's dad. Terry was having a good day today; the wheelchair was at the side of the garden, and he was managing to potter round to check on his vegetables with just the aid of a stick. James was pleased—his dad had had too few good days recently. Multiple Sclerosis was a bugger. "I'll have to get you a muzzle."

"Just showing a friendly interest," Al said, blinking would-be innocent green eyes at his friend's mother, who unfortunately for him knew quite how much to trust that particular look.

"That's what they're calling it nowadays, is it?" Laurie riposted, and James and Gillie both laughed. Laurie smiled at James. "So, what are you up to, James? Apart from studying for GCSEs, that is."

James rolled his eyes dramatically, though he was secretly pleased that Laurie cared enough to ask. "Nothing, really. Study, study, study."

"Liar," Al said mildly. "You spend all your time with that guitar. I reckon I'm losing my place as your best mate to that thing." He looked across at Laurie. "I think he goes to bed with it, you know. A love affair like no other."

"Oh, shut it, you," James said, taking one hand off the precious guitar to give his friend a shove. "Anyway, I'm working on my composition, so it's not like it's not work."

"The best sort of work is work you actually enjoy," Laurie commented. "Al's clearly just jealous. But you're still loving the guitar as much as ever then."

"God, yeah," James said fervently. "It's like... I dunno. It feels right, somehow—do you know what I mean? When I'm playing, it's like my fingers know what they should be doing. Bit like Dad and the garden, I guess. He just seems to know what to plant where and what to do to make things grow, and I'm hopeless. But my teacher shows me things on the guitar, and it makes *sense*." He flushed, embarrassed. Trying to explain how he felt about his instrument made him self-conscious. Al hadn't laughed at him, as he'd feared, when he'd said a bit about it to him—but then Al was his best mate. Laurie was...well, something different. And if Laurie laughed or teased, James didn't think he'd cope.

"That's brilliant," Laurie said, though, his expression genuinely delighted. "It sounds like you've found what's right for you, and there's nothing like that feeling. Trust me, I know."

Al ruffled James's hair. "See, it turns out you're not a weirdo. You're talented. Bastard," he added, laughing.

James was grateful for Al's interjection. It stopped the conversation getting too heavy. Talking with Laurie like this, after realising just how he felt about him...it was almost too much, in some ways.

"I wish," he said instead. "Just obsessed."

"Obsession got me a long way," Laurie assured him, looking around the garden with an expression of affection on his face. "My obsession with *Lord of the Rings*, for example, found me my best friend—and her family," he added, smiling at James, "and now my PhD. Don't knock obsession."

"I'll bear it in mind," James said, smiling back. "Speaking of which, how's the thesis going?"

Laurie sighed. "Well, it's going. I just had my last chapter ripped to shreds by my supervisor, but that's pretty much always the way. Apparently, this time, I've put in too many examples. Last chapter, it wasn't enough."

"Still searching for the pleased psychic?" James teased.

It was a long-time joke between them: at twelve, hearing the phrase "happy medium" for the first time, James had been merely bewildered, his mind quite seriously running on the idea of the paranormal. Laurie had patiently explained and had the courtesy not even to crack a smile as he did so, though they'd all laughed about it since—and the alternative term had become a standing gag.

Laurie laughed. "Apparently so. The annoying thing is my supervisor is always right. I went away and looked back through what I'd written, and every third line was an example. But still. On the plus side, I've had an article accepted by a journal this week."

"Really?" Gillie, who had wandered back to the table whilst James and Laurie chatted, settled herself comfortably in a chair and leaned across. "Which one? That's fabulous!"

Gillie was an academic herself, lecturing in English Literature, with a special interest in fantasy and science fiction, hence the shared love of the *Lord of the Rings* in both book and film version. The conversation got a bit technical for a while; James tuned out as phrases such as 'peer reviewed' and 'on the e-library catalogue' got thrown about. He concentrated instead on his guitar. He was writing a piece for his GCSE composition, and there were a few bars he wasn't happy about.

Once he settled down to music, he was lost to the world and barely noticed as Al wandered off, only registering when Al shouted, "Oh, hey, there's a bird stuck in the netting here."

"What?" demanded Terry, fired to interest as James put down his guitar to look over towards where Al was standing. "Are they after my brassicas again? I knew I was right to put those nets up."

"Its wing's all caught up, poor thing," Al said, trying to get closer to it and making the bird flap more wildly.

"Serve it right," said Terry firmly. Easy-going about most things, James's dad was undeniably overprotective when it came to his vegetables.

Laurie got to his feet and cast a laughing glance at Terry. "Probably so, but we can't just leave it there. Here, Al, move back a bit. I'll have a go."

"You?" Al looked at him doubtfully. "Aren't you a bit...big?"

Laurie stood a couple of inches over six feet and was broad-shouldered with it. Compared to Al, who was a skinny five foot six and impatiently hoping for a growth spurt which showed no sign of coming, he was definitely sizeable. And, James thought wistfully, bloody gorgeous, with his muscular physique and lazy, lopsided smile.

"Oh ye of little faith," Laurie said genially.

James watched as Laurie went carefully and quietly over to the bird, murmuring to it in an undertone. It still flapped and tried to escape, but not as manically as it had done for Al. Laurie caught it up in big gentle hands, stilling its movements with ease with one hand as he untangled the netting with the other one. It was less than a minute until he had freed the bird, which looked dazed and scurried into the undergrowth, leaving a couple of fawn-coloured feathers behind it.

"Collared dove," Terry said. "They're the worst. Still, I suppose you're right. Couldn't have left the little bugger there. Thanks, Laurie."

Gillie went over and gave Laurie a kiss. "My hero," she said. "Well done."

Laurie turned to Al. "Too big?" he asked, raising an eyebrow.

Al threw his arms up in a dramatic display of defeat. "I admit it. I was wrong. Apparently not too big at all. Having enormous hands is a great thing for rescuing small fragile creatures. Who'd have thought?"

Only James said nothing. He hated the way it had made him feel, watching Laurie concentrate so carefully on the bird. All fluttery inside, like a girl or something. Wondering what it might feel like if Laurie put those hands against him. He blinked and looked away, back at his guitar, back at anything else, and the moment passed. It didn't help him get over his crush on Laurie, though—anything but.

Still, in retrospect, that had been the best afternoon of the entire year when it came to Laurie. Most of the other occasions on which he visited, he did indeed bring Kieran. James reluctantly had to admit to himself that there was nothing intrinsically wrong with the other man except the sin that he was Laurie's boyfriend, and James was insanely jealous.

Chapter Two

THE RELATIONSHIP LASTED two years—time enough for James to get over this ridiculous attraction, he would have thought. Except somehow, he never quite did. If he didn't see Laurie for a while, James began to hope that the next time they met, he would somehow have magically got over his feelings for the older man, but it never seemed to work. Every time he saw him again, he remembered everything he loved about him. Laurie's enthusiasm for his work, even after years of working on the same thing. The way he was so large, yet so gentle. The good-humoured way he bore Al's teasing and was comfortable with anything but praise. The sparkle in his eyes when he talked. His smile. Oh god, his smile.

Laurie came to Gillie first when he broke up with Kieran. He always did come to Gillie. Somehow, James's mum was the sort of person who had this effect; people knew she was going to listen and care. She'd mothered Al more than his own mother had—Al's parents were both busy professionals, rarely home and working when they were. They seemed to see Al as more of a nuisance than anything else. Al had spent almost every weekend at James's house throughout his teens, to the point that Terry and Gillie treated him pretty much as an extra child of their own. But Laurie and Gillie's relationship was very different. Despite the age gap, Gillie had always related to Laurie as if they were equal in adult terms, and in turn, Laurie had trusted her with everything. James tried not to overhear when Laurie told Gillie that he and Kieran were history; he even tried not to be pleased, but he couldn't help it. He was eighteen now; it wouldn't be inappropriate to date Laurie. Not right now, of course—not just after he'd broken up with Kieran—but sometime.

"I know what you're thinking," Al said to him a couple of weeks later as they sat watching a DVD of a Japanese film with what James privately considered downright confusing subtitles. Al had seen it before, but he insisted it was a classic and had forced James to watch it with him.

"What?" James asked defensively.

"Laurie," Al said. "You are still hung up on him, aren't you? Yes, I thought so. Just checking."

"Oh, shut up."

"I haven't even said it yet."

"No, but you're right. He's single." James looked at Al pleadingly. "I have to do something."

"Not two weeks after he's broken up with his boyfriend. Wasn't he actually living with Kieran?"

"Yes." James did not say how much he had loathed it when the two had moved in together. He didn't need to. Al knew. Al knew everything—it had never been possible for James to keep secrets from Al. "And no, not after two weeks. But..."

"Yeah." Al sighed. "God, I hope I never fall in love. What a bloody nightmare."

"Sometimes." But James's face was blazing with excitement. "What if he says yes, though, Al? Maybe...maybe we could be together, after all."

"Yeah." Al clapped his friend on the back. "I hope so. Just give it a while, yeah? And shush now—there's a good bit in the film just coming up. You're going to love it."

James grinned and subsided. But Al's advice was good. He would wait—at least a little while.

In the end, it was one week after his nineteenth birthday, which fell at the beginning of September, and two weeks before James was due to go to university when he spoke to Laurie. Long enough after finishing school to make it safe to be out as gay—though for Laurie's sake, James would have risked it anyway, even before leaving—and four months after Laurie's breakup with Kieran. James had been considering saying something the whole summer, but there was always a reason not to: it hadn't been long enough since Kieran, or Al was there and he didn't want an audience, or James's parents were monopolising Laurie, or it was the wrong type of rain, or whatever it was. But James had only two weeks until he was moving away to Guildford to attend the University of Surrey, and it was now or never.

Laurie and he were sitting in the garden. They'd been there for about an hour, chatting. James had been telling about the university course he'd chosen. He'd picked music, of course—he was still a passionate musician, though he didn't want to perform as a career, being fatally shy for such a profession—and he went into a few of the details about the halls of residence.

"I suppose you're going to be leaving pretty soon," Laurie said. He looked at James. "I'll miss you. Won't seem right without you here."

James felt his heart thump. He had to take this moment. There wasn't going to be another one. "I'll miss you too."

Before he could think too hard about it and change his mind yet again, he leaned across the wooden bench they were both sitting on and kissed Laurie firmly on the mouth. For a few seconds, Laurie's mouth opened willingly underneath his, and Laurie's hand went to his shoulder; then, as quickly as he'd started, Laurie pulled away.

"James..."

"Let me," James pleaded.

He had a bit of experience with kissing—over the past year, he'd snogged a few blokes, anonymously, in London, dragging Al—who had come out as bisexual around that time—to gay bars in parts of town where he was least likely to bump into anyone from school. Not to mention, he'd kissed a few girls when he was in year twelve in a desperate, doomed-to-failure attempt not to be gay—and to get over a certain man of his acquaintance—but this was different. This was Laurie, and Laurie mattered.

And Laurie was looking anything but pleased at being kissed. In fact, he was looking positively terrified. "James, we can't—I can't—I—"

"I'm in love with you, you know," James said quietly. He hadn't intended to say it; certainly not that bluntly, but it had come out.

Laurie shook his head. "No. No, you're not. You're...you're just... I'm too old, and your parents... And this is such a bad idea. Look. Let's forget this. You're about to go to uni. I get it. There'll be lots of blokes there, and if you've just discovered you're gay, and I'm the only gay bloke you know...there will be loads there, and..."

"It's not like that." James sat back, though. He didn't know why he was continuing to speak. Clearly, Laurie wasn't interested, but he was damned if he was going to let Laurie patronise him with his 'only gay in the village' spiel. "I've known I'm gay since I was fourteen years old, for fuck's sake. As for you being the only bloke I know who likes men, don't flatter yourself. Al does, for a start—he likes girls too, but guys as well. If you're going to turn me down," he said, his voice coldly furious, "do it honestly. Don't be a coward and put it all onto me. I've just turned nineteen. I'm not a kid. I love you, and if you don't feel the same, have the common decency to just tell me."

Laurie looked pale and clammy and uncomfortable. "I'm sorry," he said. "I was crass. But this—us—is not an option. I still say you're about to go to uni, and even if everything else were right, even if I—I felt anything for you anyway, it wouldn't be a good time. You don't want to go to uni with a new boyfriend hanging round your neck like a millstone. You want to go and have fun. And I'm...I'm not the right person anyway. Not for you. I'm sorry."

James didn't know what he looked like, but he was pretty sure it wasn't his best look. He felt as if someone had just reached inside him and yanked his guts around with their bare hands. In a distant sort of way, he was quite impressed that he was just sitting there, not throwing up or crying or god knew what. But it hurt too much for him to care much about appearances.

"Well," he said stiffly, forcing himself to stand up, willing his knees not to tremble beneath him. "I think that's fairly final."

He turned away and walked into the house, and he could feel Laurie's eyes on his back the whole way.

Of course, he couldn't control it when he was alone. The moment he was in his room, James found himself sobbing, face down on the bed. And he was still crying when Al arrived nearly an hour later. He tried to stop as he heard his bedroom door bang open, but it was difficult to stop all in a second after so long. Al dropped his bag with a heavy thump and was over with him immediately.

"James. Jamie?"

James gulped and took a deep breath, scrubbing his arm across his face to try to get rid of the traces of tears. "I'm a fucking idiot," he said unclearly, trying to remember how to breathe normally and wishing his nose wasn't so blocked.

"I know," said Al, giving him a hug. Al was always tactile. The tone was more gentle than the words, as was typical with Al. "In what particular way this time? You're going to have to talk to someone about it, you know. Might as well be me. It usually is."

He was right. It usually was. It *always* was, in fact. And Al knew all about James's feelings for Laurie, so that part was hardly going to be a surprise.

"Fuck." James sat up and sniffed hard. His voice was gravelly from sobbing, and he felt hot and sticky all over. "Hang on a sec. Let me go and wash my face. I feel a mess."

"You look it," Al agreed. Come to that, James had seen Al looking better, too. His face was usually pale, but it was quite white.

James got up and washed and returned to the room. "Sorry," he said, sounding more like himself, to his relief.

"Spill," Al said succinctly.

"Laurie."

"Oh." Nine years of close friendship meant that often not everything needed to be said aloud. The two young men looked at each other for a moment. "You said something then."

James gave a mirthless laugh. "I kissed him."

"Well, that would do it. Not a success?"

"He tried to tell me it was because he was the only gay guy I knew," James said. "I outed you, by the way," he added. "To make a point."

"I didn't know I was in," Al said casually.

Unlike James, who had agonised over his sexuality, making absolutely certain not to tell anyone he was gay until his A levels were finished, Al had quite candidly informed everyone at the beginning of year thirteen that he was bisexual and therefore up for offers from both guys and girls. In a school where 'gay' and 'homo' were the insults of choice, it had been a brave or possibly foolhardy decision. To James's rueful amazement, however, Al had got away with it, though he readily admitted he'd been grateful for James's unswerving support. He'd had a number of gross comments thrown his way, certainly, but insults were water off a duck's back to Al. He still hadn't seemed to have much trouble pulling, though any guys that he'd been with had not been from the school itself. The girls hadn't seemed to care much, however—unless it had made Al more attractive. James wasn't sure.

"I didn't think you'd be too bothered," James agreed. He covered his face with his hands. "Oh, god, it was such a fuck-up. He treated me like I was some idiot kid." He sighed. "I told him I was in love with him, too."

Al reached over and ruffled his hair. "Blimey, you really went for it, didn't you?" he said gently. "He's the idiot not to be interested. I'm sorry, mate."

James felt his eyes prickling again and blinked the tears fiercely away. "I've been in love with him for so damn long, and he just doesn't care. And there's nothing I can do about it, is there?"

"No." Al's voice was sad. "There isn't. I wish I could change it for you, Jamie. I'm sorry." He took a deep breath. "Want to hear about my woes?"

James looked over at him. So Al really had been looking pale. It was extremely unlike Al to be upset about anything, which meant that it had to be serious.

"What's up?" he asked, preparing to give Al his full attention.

"What, you mean apart from the fact I'm now in the interesting position of Laurie potentially being one of my lecturers"—Al was going to be attending Laurie and Gillie's university, where Laurie had just got a post as a sessional lecturer in Film Studies, Al's degree subject—"and my wanting to tell him he's an utter wanker?"

James gave a half-hearted smile. "Yeah, apart from that."

"My parents are moving to the States."

"Whaaat?" James stared at him. "When?"

"Six weeks."

Al looked a little bit lost, and James wasn't surprised. Al wasn't close to his parents—they had always been too busy and never appeared to care much for him anyway. James's mum had commented once in James's hearing that she couldn't understand why they'd ever had a child in the first place, "unless it was something to tick off a list of 'achievements'". Al himself had said on more than one occasion that they wished they'd never had him, though James had just put that down as hyperbole. But to discover they were moving to the other side of the world and were going so soon, leaving Al alone in England must have been a shock.

"Six weeks? Seriously? Isn't that a bit sudden?"

Al nodded. "Apparently they've known for a while, but they were waiting to tell me until I'd got the uni accommodation sorted out. The house has been sold—I'm so glad they bothered to tell me that the house I grew up in had been sold—and Dad's got a job in Florida. Earning masses, apparently, like that's the most important thing." He gave a small smile. "Oh, and they don't think there's much point my going over there before the summer, as they'll be getting themselves sorted out, and anyway 'think of the plane costs' because it's not like they're loaded or anything. D'you think your mum would have me for Christmas?"

"Sure she would," James said, answering the easy bit first. Then, returning for a second to his own problems. "Shit, Laurie always comes for Christmas. If I never see him again, it'll be too soon."

"Fuck him." Al made a face. "Or rather, don't. Fuck everyone else at uni, and by the time you get back, you won't care."

"That's what he thinks I'm going to do," James said rather grimly. "Once I've discovered he's not the only gay person ever, obviously."

"Who cares what he thinks?" Al said, ignoring the fact that James quite clearly did. "You've spent the past god knows how many years mooning about after him, and it stops here. Okay? Sleep with them. Sleep with them all. See if you care."

James nodded, knowing he wouldn't do it. "I just...always thought—hoped—Laurie would be my first, you know? Sorry, this is probably TMI, but—"

"No such thing as TMI with me, mate," Al said cheerfully and with undoubted truth.

"Well," James confessed, needing to tell someone, "it's just that whenever I've thought about having sex, it's with Laurie. With him fucking me. I've—Oh god, why couldn't he just want me?" He knew how pathetic he sounded and could have said all of this to no one but Al.

"Because he's a bloody idiot," Al said. He paused, but James could feel that it was a pause and not that Al had finished speaking.

"What?"

"Well," said Al slowly, "there's more than one way of having sex, you know."

"Blow jobs," James said.

"Yeah, those too, but that's not what I meant. I mean, well—there's no reason someone has to fuck you, you know."

"Huh?"

"You could always do them." Al grinned. "I've tried both, and believe me, they both have their merits. So Laurie won't fuck you? You can go out and fuck someone else. I mean, the best option is just to forget the bastard and find someone else you want to fuck you. But failing that..."

James knew Al was right, and what he really ought to do was move on, move forward. Get the hell over it. He also knew that wasn't going to happen—not yet. James couldn't, truthfully, imagine it happening at any time. He'd been in love with Laurie for two and a half years. It wasn't exactly a sudden bolt from the blue. But it was like Al to know that and to offer another suggestion. James couldn't imagine having sex with anyone who wasn't Laurie...well, he could, but he couldn't say it held the same appeal. Or any appeal at all right now, in all honesty. But to do something different to the thing he'd been fantasising about—okay, why not admit it?—wanking off to for years seemed at least a little more possible, somehow.

"Thanks," he said. "I'll bear it in mind." Meanwhile, however, there was Al's issue. James couldn't get his head around the fact that Al's parents had basically just told him that they had no interest in seeing him for a year. He'd known they were cold, but that was fucking heartless. "Mum always wants you here," he said, changing the subject abruptly. "So do I, come to that. Why are we going to different universities, Al?"

Al's face lit into his wicked smile. "So you can discover that you can cope without me, of course," he said. "I know it'll be hard, but—"

"Oh, fuck off," said James. "God knows what trouble you'll get into without me to sort it out for you"—a not altogether unreasonable comment, given their past history together; James's sturdy common sense had pulled Al out of a number of less-than-optimal situations in their school days—"but *I'll* be fine."

"You can always come back odd weekends, anyway," Al said. "It's not like you're all that far away."

James thought about Laurie, and his face hardened. "Or you can come to me," he said. "I'll be glad to get away." There was definitely bitterness in his voice.

Al punched him lightly. "Yeah, yeah, you're better off without Laurie, and I'm better off without my parents, and everything in the garden is pretty bloody sucky right now, isn't it?"

James smiled reluctantly. Al could always cheer him up, at least to a degree. He had Al. He had parents who cared for him. He could do this. He could get over Laurie. Maybe, maybe, things would be okay.

Chapter Three

JAMES DID HIS best. He really did. He was one of the first sign-ups of the freshers for the LGBT Society at university. He made the effort to go out a lot, though it wasn't entirely his thing; and he found a number of friends. What was more, he genuinely loved his course. But he wasn't happy, despite his claims to the contrary. Al texted him regularly, but James's responses were brief and sporadic; it wasn't until he got an email from Al that he allowed himself to realise how much he was missing his best friend.

To: jamescape224@gmail.com
From: almeister-hitchins@gmail.com
Subject: Earth Calling Jamie
Hey Jamie,
Never realised before now that your name could be differently parsed to read 'jam escape'. Why didn't I ever think of this at school? Bugger it.

Hope all's going well with you. You're bloody crap at responding to texts, you know. Why the fuck do you have a phone if you aren't going to use it? My course looks amazing, and I've already met loads of people. Got off with four people already—I've made it clear I'm not in the market for a relationship, and it's incredible how many people are cool with that. It's great. Doing a module on music in film, so you should be impressed by that!

Went to see your parents the other day—your dad's bought me a bookcase and a cupboard, of all things; wants me to dump all the stuff I can't take to uni at your place now my oldies are sodding off abroad. Doesn't say much, your dad, but when he does, it's to the point. You got all the luck when it came to parents.

Don't be a stranger!

Al

James sighed. He missed his parents, as well as Al, even though it was thoroughly uncool to admit it. And Laurie. He'd spent the final two weeks of the holiday avoiding Laurie; but now, when he couldn't see him again even had he wanted to, he regretted it. Of course, it would be horrendously awkward if he were to see him, after last time. James's mother had gathered that something was up between the two of them, but James had refused to explain and begged her not to ask Laurie. He knew she wouldn't—his mum was good like that. But it had cast a shadow over the last of his time at home, and suddenly everything seemed miles away. Probably because it was.

Still, he wasn't going to admit that to Al—from the sound of it, Al was having a whale of a time. He clicked reply.

To: almeister-hitchins@gmail.com
From: jamescape224@gmail.com
Subject: re: Earth Calling Jamie
Almeister? Seriously? What were you thinking? And all I can say is, thank god the jam thing didn't occur to you at school. I had the piss ripped out of me enough just for putting up with you without anything else added.

Course here looks great, too, and I took your advice and joined the LGBT society. Feels bloody weird being out after so many years hiding it. You'll be entertained to know that I've got a module called 'film music' this year, too. Great minds—or possibly fools...

Good old Dad. Please tell me he didn't try to load you up with the last of the French beans or something to take back to your uni halls with you. It kills me the way he does that to everyone who visits.

I'd say I'm missing you, but I'd be a big fat liar. God, isn't it nice to be out of school at long last?

James

Of course, it was indeed nice to be out of school. And to be studying something that James was passionately interested in. And he made quite a few friends, both from his music course and from the LGBT society, which was full of fun and interesting people. He even—tentatively, because he knew deep inside that he was still hung up on Laurie—dated. There was a nice guy called Carl in the society; Czech, with a daft sense of humour and an obsession with geckos. James and he started going out, and in early November, ended up in bed together. Sex was good, James decided, afterwards, though not all it was hyped up to be. He couldn't help wondering what it was that Al saw in it that made him so keen to hop into bed with whomsoever he could find. It got considerably better after a few attempts, however— with James topping, as advised by Al—but when James realised that Carl was falling seriously for him, he had to break it off. No matter how much he wished it wasn't true, he couldn't get Laurie out of his head.

He went home at Christmas time single, but sexually experienced; and knowing that he couldn't get into another relationship unless or until his feelings about Laurie changed drastically. Al, predictably, got this out of him within twenty-four hours of his return, and he rolled his eyes but was otherwise sympathetic.

"Oh well, if you can't, you can't. Any ideas what you're going to do about Laurie over Christmas? Gillie informs me I'm on your floor again."

Al's room was the one which was always taken over when guests—which usually meant Laurie—stayed. Fair enough that it was so, Al had pointed out once, given that he wasn't actually a member of the household, no matter how much he felt like one. Though James had pointed out in return that chucking him out was much more 'homelike' than keeping him in the same room would be. At any rate, Al had been sleeping on a mattress on James's floor for so much of his life that it barely needed a second mention. Now that Al's parents had moved abroad, however, Laurie was going to have to put up with a lot more of Al's belongings scattered around the room he would be sleeping in, but James suspected he wouldn't mind that much. A hell of a lot of it was film-related; Laurie should feel right at home, James thought ironically.

James grimaced. "Not really. Pretend it didn't happen? It's either that or hide every time he comes into a room and—"

"You know I'll rip the piss out of you mercilessly if you do that," Al finished for him.

James gave him a shove. "That was not how that sentence was supposed to finish, no. I'm better than that." He made a moue with his lips. "And it's not exactly going to convince him that I'm all grown up if I'm running away, is it?"

Al sighed. "Oh, Jamie," he said, but his criticism went no further than that.

It seemed as if Laurie, too, was quite happy to pretend that the kiss the previous summer had never happened, to James's relief. There was still a residual awkwardness between them. Their old, relaxed friendship was less in evidence, and they talked only about general mundane topics, but it was enough for now. More than enough, because James found that his new sexual experience meant that his fantasies about Laurie could be considerably more accurate and explicit. Sharing a room with Al meant that he didn't have a lot of occasions on which to put this new information to its most obvious use, but seeing Laurie again had only served to remind James of how strong, indeed, his feelings still were for the older man. He'd half hoped that things might have changed—*oh, how many times had he hoped that about Laurie in his life, James wondered*—but it seemed it was not so. Al poked him on occasion when he was staring too obviously—"Looking moony again, Jamie. Stoppit!"—and James struggled through the Christmas holidays without embarrassing himself too much.

It was great to be back with his parents and Al, anyway. James's mother loved Christmas—loved having her family around her—for she counted both Al and Laurie as pretty much family—and celebrating with good food, fun, and decorations. She was an amazing cook, and James enjoyed cooking almost as much as his mum did, so he and Gillie spent hours in the kitchen companionably chopping and dicing and baking, while he introduced her to the new music he'd discovered during his first term at uni. And whilst James still thought Al's parents were on course for shittiest parents ever, given that they'd told their only son they didn't want to see him over Christmas, he couldn't help admitting that it worked out nicely in his favour. Having Al around all the time was—well, it just felt right. He'd have died rather than told Al that explicitly; the nearest they had come being James's mild, "Bloody weird not having you around at uni. Keep checking to see what trouble you've got yourself into and then remembering you aren't there."

"Yeah, well," Al had retorted, "I keep waiting to catch one of your disapproving looks, and all. But at least I text you."

"Only because you drunk-text me."

"And?"

"Clearly I just don't drink as much as you."

Al had raised an eyebrow. "Ah, so you've been making up for it this holidays? That explains a lot."

The conversation had disintegrated into a fight, only stopping when one of the decorations in the living room looked under threat. Nonetheless, James was pretty sure Al wasn't too sad to see him either; and he could have hugged his best friend when, on Christmas night, he gave James's mum a squeeze and said with palpable truth, "Best Christmas ever. Thanks for having me here, Gillie."

James had known his mother was fond of Al, but as she was holding him close, he was pretty sure that Al had not seen the unexpected delight in her face when he spoke. James was, he reckoned, pretty bloody lucky, all in all, Laurie notwithstanding.

THE REST OF the year passed well enough. James enjoyed uni; he enjoyed the more grown-up feel of it, the way he had to make his own decisions about what work to do and when. No one was going to force him into anything: if he didn't get the work done, his grades would suffer, but it was up to him. He found halls living a bit stressful, side by side with so many other students, and was looking forward to the following year, when he would be in a shared house with just three other students—one male, two female, none straight, so that his friend Jenny was threatening to label it the Rainbow House, except that the other three had threatened to kill her if she tried any such thing. It wasn't that he was antisocial, per se, but that he preferred small gatherings to parties—and he definitely preferred being able to sleep without someone down the corridor playing terrible music at 2:00 a.m. James had spent many a restless night wondering whether the lack of sleep or the appalling musical taste of some of his corridor mates was the worst part. He still hadn't found a definitive answer to that one.

The summer was curious. Al was in America for eight weeks with his parents, and James took the chance to spend some more time with his own parents, his dad especially. Terry's MS was noticeably worse than it had been the summer before, though he was coping with his usual lack of drama.

"Bad years happen," he said with a shrug, ignoring the fact that the lesions he got were permanent.

But James knew that his father had improved again in the past; with any luck, it would happen once more. Meantime, it was good to spend time with him. His father was a quiet man, easy to be with. They could sit in silence or watch a TV programme and make occasional comments relating to it. It was a strange way, perhaps, for a nineteen-year-old to spend his summer, James thought, but not a bad one. He got a part-time job shelf-stacking at a local shop—not big enough to be a supermarket, not small enough to be a corner shop—and was happy enough pootling around. Laurie was around fairly regularly, and James was comfortable enough with that. The conversation rarely progressed beyond "Hi James. How's it doing?"

"Yeah, not too bad. Got a shift at the shop in a while. I'd better get ready."

But that was all to the good. Without Al there, James didn't dare spend too much time in Laurie's presence, in case he was gazing wistfully at the other man in a hideously embarrassing fashion, without realising it. There were no two ways about it—

he fancied the bloody arse off the man, still. And when Laurie smiled or said something more meaningful than "how are you?" James had a horrendous urge to ask him out, or do something equally ill-judged. Laurie played havoc with his inhibitions, so it made more sense to keep out of the way. Al, when James emailed him about the situation, agreed fervently with this decision.

They emailed quite a lot that summer, James and Al, and Skyped occasionally. James gathered more from what Al didn't say than what he did that he was not enjoying himself. He said, briefly, that his parents were very busy—the first time they'd seen him in a year, James thought grimly, and they were 'very busy'— so that he hadn't seen much of them. It seemed they lived in a large house, but in a rather out of the way area; without a car, Al was finding it difficult to get out much. *My lecturers are going to love me next year, though—what I don't know about the courses I'm taking isn't worth knowing. Heck, give it another couple of weeks, and I could probably* teach *the courses.* James realised guiltily that he was definitely not quite so up on his preparation, and he should probably give it a look-over. He emailed Al, telling him that he was having a freakishly good influence—*the sort which probably only happens when you're thousands of miles away from me.*

It was good to see Al on his return, however—though James had to do a double take to recognise his best friend. Al had spent the whole of his first year growing his hair; it had looked good on him, especially combined with his now trademark look of black jeans and fandom- or geek-related T-shirts also predominantly in black. The Al he met at the airport, however, had an almost militarily short haircut and wore grey trousers and a blue shirt. James's gaze quite literally passed over him the first moment he saw him; might have done again if Al hadn't caught sight of him in return and dropped all his belongings to yell, "Hey, Jamie!" with a wide and very familiar smile.

"Al." James pulled his best friend into a big hug. "You look...different."

He picked up one of Al's heavy cases and left the other to his friend.

Al grimaced. "Godawful, isn't it? Still, anything to oblige the 'rents." James gave a snort at this, and Al grinned sheepishly. "Yeah, well, I thought I'd make the effort, anyway. Especially as they weren't going to let me out of the house unless I did."

"*What?*"

"You know what they're like. Are we taking the bus into London?"

"Yes, and don't change the subject."

"They didn't feel that they could introduce me to their friends, looking the way I did," Al said briefly, hauling his case behind him.

"Did you want to be introduced to their friends?" James asked dryly.

"I wanted to be let out of the house, to be honest. To go anywhere. Don't ask me what Florida's like, Jamie; I didn't really see much of it. Warm, in my parents' back garden...sorry...yard. But I had to stay decently dressed because I didn't want to offend the gardener, did I?" Al sighed. "No, it was fine. It was. I did my duty, and I don't think my mother said out loud once that she wished I didn't exist. I'm calling that a win. At least they'd admitted to some of their friends that they actually had a son. I did wonder, the first week, when they said that they thought it might be better if I just stayed in the house and 'acclimatised'."

"Bloody hell," said James.

Had Al's parents seriously always been like this? He'd seemed to spend most of his time at outs with them in some way, and James had never liked them much, the few times they'd met. Their attitude had seemed to be, if James was totally honest, that if he was a friend of their son's, there must be something wrong with him. But James had put it down to his own paranoia; his mother had said that they were always perfectly civil to her. "Yeah," Al had said cynically, "they would be. They don't want her to stop taking me off their hands, do they?"

"Oh well. I'm home now, duty done. And don't," Al added, glaring at James, "ask me if it was military duty. I know all about the haircut, and if you don't think I'm humiliated enough by it, then trust me, I am. And we've got second year coming up soon, but I've got a couple of weeks of messing around with you first, and believe me, I intend to make the most of it."

Chapter Four

SECOND YEAR WAS good. James thrived in the shared house and was falling more and more in love with his course. He was also persuaded, somewhat against his better judgement, to try dating again. Friedrich was on the same course as James's housemate Jenny (English Literature), and it was clear after he'd spent a lot of time around at their house studying with Jenny that he was interested in James. Fred was nice, and he was fun to be around. It didn't hurt that he was tall with light brown hair, either...a bit like someone else that James knew. Not quite as tall or broad as Laurie—an inch or so shorter than James himself, where Laurie was taller—but decent-looking and clearly very interested in James. Having spent the summer pining after someone who was quite clearly *not* interested in him, James couldn't help acknowledging to himself that his ego was soothed by having someone else show an interest in him. The sex was better than it had been with Carl, even—and much, much better than the one-night stand that James had tried in the summer term—and James began to feel a bit hopeful about the relationship...until he went home for Christmas and saw Laurie again.

Wanking in the shower to thoughts of his mother's best friend when he had a boyfriend who was very keen on him was... It made James feel dirty and unpleasant. Not for the first time, he wondered how Al managed to juggle more than one partner—for, whilst Al had one-night stands like they were going out of fashion, he also had several people with whom he slept on a more regular basis, albeit on the understanding that there was nothing serious going on between them—without feeling horrible about it. When James went back to uni and found himself fantasising about Laurie whilst actually having sex with Fred, he broke it off. There were some levels to which he was not prepared to descend. Fred was a lovely guy, and he deserved much better. He had to put up with the sad-eyed looks from Jenny, but that was to be preferred to the guilt. And when Fred started dating their other housemate, Peter, just before Easter, James was genuinely delighted for them both.

But oh, how he missed the sex.

It annoyed James massively when he first realised that. Damn it, he'd managed for years with Al having sex like a blasted maniac, and James hadn't been bothered—hadn't been interested, if it wasn't going to be Laurie—in the slightest. He had enjoyed a good wank—he wasn't abnormal, for fuck's sake—but he hadn't felt any need to have sex with another person. Hadn't. Ha, how *that* had changed. It was even worse knowing that Fred and Peter were probably having extremely satisfying sex in the room next door, and that if James wasn't hung up on someone he'd fancied since he was sixteen years old, he might actually have been able to be doing the same. He had no regrets about breaking up with Fred; he could have done nothing else in the circumstances. But bloody hell, the sex had been *good*, and James missed it. For the second time, he tried a one-night stand, and for the second time, he regretted it; he felt no connection to the man and didn't enjoy what they did together, which never even got as far as intercourse. James could only be grateful for that but, nonetheless, went home for the Easter holidays irritable and sexually frustrated.

It took Al—oh, about five minutes?—to work out that James wasn't on top form. Al himself was practically bouncing off the ceiling; apparently he'd had the term of a lifetime. James wasn't sure whether it was the drinking and fucking—both of which, it seemed, there had been plenty—or the Film Studies course. He suspected that in truth it was the latter, though Al would never admit it, of course. Owning to enjoying university was one thing—and almost expected. Owning to enjoying it predominantly because you loved the work...that was quite another. James reminded himself to tease Al mercilessly about that at the next possible occasion, even though he had to admit that he too was rather enthused by the modules he was taking. Composition was the best one he'd ever done—he actively looked forward to the seminars, and revelled in the way his new knowledge was affecting (improving) the pieces he'd always written.

"Come on," Al said bluntly that evening, when they'd retired to James's room with a bottle of wine that James's mum had handed them. "Spit it out, whatever it is."

"What?"

"Oh, don't give me that," said Al, rolling his eyes and pouring wine haphazardly into two glasses. "Something's pissing you off. You've got the 'James Cape pissed off face' on, and it's been there ever since you got home." He considered. "Well, not 'pissed off' so much as... I dunno what it is. But you're upset by something. All this 'blah blah, uni's great' stuff is fine. That's fab. So what's up?"

"Oh, bugger you, Al Hitchins," James said with resignation. "Am I really that transparent?"

He grabbed one of the glasses from Al before his friend could spill it as he waved his arms around to make a point. It was a constant hazard with Al, who spoke with his whole body, not just his mouth.

"Is it your ex getting together with your housemate?" Al asked, sipping from the other glass of wine. Then, "Bugger, this wine is much nicer than the stuff I buy. Hope your mum doesn't mind me replacing it with a five-quid bottle from Morrison's, because there's no way I'm going to be able to afford something this decent. You should stop me stealing your parents' wine; you really should."

"Yeah, cos I'm not drinking it at all," James pointed out with sarcasm. "And it's not like Mum handed it to you and said 'Try this one' or anything. She doesn't want us to replace it. She doesn't care."

Al gave a slightly twitchy nod. James knew that now he was older, Al felt somewhat as if he abused the Capes' hospitality, given the amount of time he spent there. He knew, too, that his parents loved having Al around; but somehow, Al had never quite been able to believe it.

"Suppose so. So, is that the problem? Not the wine, I mean, the bloke?"

"No," James said. A pause. "Yes. Sort of."

"Oh well, that's helped." Sarcasm at its highest from Al.

"I'm pleased. I really am," said James with utter sincerity. "They make a decent couple, and I'm the one who dumped Fred, after all."

"Ye-es," said Al, looking vaguely disapproving. He knew precisely—well, not precisely—not about the fantasising about Laurie during sex bit, which James had kept firmly to himself, thank you very much, but he knew the general details of why that relationship, like the last, had gone west. "Not that I particularly wish him ill or anything, but... If Laurie had a mysterious tragic accident, do you think you'd finally get over the bastard? Because from what you were saying, Fred was a reasonable enough bloke."

"Yeah, and I can now lay claim to having kept a relationship for two months, which is more than you've ever done," James shot back.

"Thing is, I don't want to."

James grimaced. "Nor do I. At least..."

"Not if it's not Laurie." Al groaned. "I know, I know. Stubborn tosser, aren't you? Okay, so you're pleased Fred's seeing someone else. That's not the problem. Except that it 'sort of' is. So what is it?"

James could feel himself blushing. It was one thing to be missing having sex, and another to admit it out loud. "I'm not... It's just... I don't like..."

"Last of the great communicators. Drink some more wine, Jamie," Al advised. "You'll tell me when you're sloshed enough, anyway."

"Oh, fuck off," said James, knowing it was true. He nonetheless took Al's advice—and a large gulp of very potable wine. Al was right; this was definitely nicer than the wine James drank at uni. "I just am a bit...weirded out by the thought of them having sex in the room next door to mine, you know? When Fred and I..."

Al sniggered. Positively, he sniggered. "Console yourself the other two in the house are lesbians, so he can't do the rounds any further," he said, grinning.

"He's not *you*," James said pointedly, which only made Al's grin wider.

"No. In that case you might have to worry," he said mischievously. "It's always worth testing to make absolutely sure you're not bi, after all."

James gave him a two-fingered salute for this remark. "Anyway, that's not the problem either. I mean, he can have sex with who the hell he likes. It's not that I resent him having a sex life. It's just..." He sighed. "Well, look, the trouble is, sex is...well, way better than wanking, frankly. It was fine when I didn't know, but now I do..."

Al was outright laughing at him now. James glared. "Sorry," Al apologised, not sounding sorry in the slightest. "It's the tone of injured surprise that got me. But yeah, they're not in the same league." He considered. "Well," he said thoughtfully, "shitty sex is considerably worse, but—"

"Ugh, I know," James acknowledged, thinking of the failed one-night stand he hadn't quite had. "But with someone you can practise a few times with, it's...well..."

"Yeah."

"But I can't," James said pathetically. "How can I get into a relationship with someone when I'm always thinking about Laurie? About his—"

"Okay, okay, I'm not sure I need details," Al said hastily. "Remember I'm going to have to look him in the face on Easter Day...and I want to make sure I *am* looking at his face and not looking at his bits and thinking about what you've been saying about—"

"Right, you can shut up too," James interrupted in turn. "Thing is, that doesn't leave me a lot of options. And it's...bloody frustrating, quite frankly."

"Well, you could always sleep with me," Al suggested.

James's first reaction to this remarkable offer was to fall about laughing. Al's green eyes danced with amusement in response.

"Al Hitchins," James said at last, "did you just proposition me?"

Fortunately, it was almost impossible to offend Al. He grinned. "It just seemed like an obvious solution," he said, shrugging. "I know the score with Laurie; it doesn't have to be a one-night stand, and without being rude, Jamie, the day I want a relationship with you is the day I fear for my sanity." He thought for a second. "To be fair, the day I want a relationship with anyone is the day I fear for my sanity," he corrected himself.

James smiled at his friend. "Fair enough. But no. It'd be too bloody weird. Thanks, though."

"Not a problem," Al said casually. "The offer's there if you change your mind." His face had the mischievous look in it that James knew so well. "And I'm bloody good, you know."

James snorted at that. "Modest, with it." He gave Al a shove. "Seriously, thanks. But I'll work something out."

By the end of the summer term, however, what James had worked out was a long-term relationship with his right hand and not a lot else. He knew that Jason, from his composition module, would have gone out with him in a flash if he'd asked; he also knew that he'd never ask. How could he, when the only person he could think about seriously was Laurie?

He hated himself for that. He hated Laurie for that quite a lot, too. Twenty-one fucking months—not that he was counting— since Laurie had turned him down, and he was still hung up on the guy. Well. He had been since he was sixteen years old; why not admit it? He was a fucking lunatic, was James Cape. Obsessing about a man who saw him as something like a kid brother. The trouble was, it didn't matter how many times James had this conversation with himself, he still couldn't stop loving Laurie. And, quite frankly, it sucked.

James was also horny as hell and with nothing to do with it. Oh, he'd had yet another one-nighter—and gone all the way this time—but that had just left him feeling grim and unclean, as someone he didn't give a toss about rubbed intimate body parts against his own. All he knew for certain was that it was not something he was going to do again, *ever*. How Al could stand it all the time, James didn't know. But it clearly worked for him, and James was pleased for him. He was, moreover, evidently going mad, as he was seriously thinking about taking his best friend up on his offer.

This year, Al was staying all summer with the Capes. Gillie had made it clear that she considered it Al's home, and although Al's parents had said that they would pay for him to go over to America if he wished, it had been evident that it was obligation and not a desire to see him, which had caused them to offer. The offer, even then, had been given grudgingly, as if they were conferring a favour on their only child by making it.

"Ironic, really, that your mum wants me more than mine does," Al commented to James with a shrug; and James didn't know how to respond to that one, because it was true. "Still," Al added, "it beats sitting in an empty house in Florida, dying of boredom, which was last summer's joy. I might even get a summer job—you never know."

And he did. There was an independent wine shop not far from the university, and Al bagged himself some shifts there. Fenella, the owner, usually had other students working for her, but they were going home for the summer, so Al suggested that he take the place of one of them for the duration—a situation which suited everyone well. Al's student loans were enough that he could avoid having to get a job during term time, so long as he was careful—and Al was surprisingly careful with money—so he would happily give up the job come the end of the summer holidays; and the cash meantime would allow him to pay Gillie and Terry some rent over the summer, as he was insisting on doing despite their objections.

"I'm not cheap to feed," he informed Gillie firmly, and James knew that his mum wasn't able to deny that. For a comparatively small young man—Al had finally grown to a slender five feet eight inches, which wasn't diminutive per se but was definitely small compared to James's broader six feet—Al ate like a horse.

Plus, Terry was taking early retirement from his job that summer, too, so although money wasn't a major concern, it was undeniably going to be different from here on in. The MS wasn't improving, and it seemed stupid—James's mother said—for his dad to be using all of his energy on work and never getting to have any fun out of life. James knew his dad wasn't that keen on his job anyway—he'd had to move slowly down the scale, thanks to his health problems deteriorating over the past five years, and was now working at a level considerably below his abilities. So James couldn't help agreeing with his mum that it was best that Dad retired. But it did mean that Al was more determined than ever not to be a burden on the family which had taken him in with so much enthusiasm and love.

James and Al spent the first couple of days back catching up on everything which had been going on. Al had tried his hand at film-making and was immediately passionate about it. His final year project would be to create a short film from scratch, and he was almost frenzied with the amount of ideas he already had. James, meanwhile, was looking into both the composition of music—because he couldn't help himself; he'd always composed, and he suspected he always would—and the more realistic career possibility of teaching the guitar. He was already being paid by another student—mostly in beer and chips—to teach the basics to her, and to his surprise he was enjoying it immensely. It was not until the third day, therefore, that James brought up the thorny subject of sex.

"Al," he said, as they sat on the bed that Tuesday evening, "do you remember having a conversation about sex last Easter?"

Al threw him a disbelieving look. "Jamie, I spend half my life talking about sex. When I'm not in seminars, anyway. Actually," he added thoughtfully, "even when I am. Films with fast cars—metaphors for sex. Films with dark corridors or tunnels—metaphors for sex. Means pretty much all action and horror flicks can be seen as carefully disguised porn if you look closely enough. Anyway, sorry. Conversation with you. At Easter. Sex." He thought back. "We talked about..." He stopped suddenly and looked more closely at James. "Oh. *That* conversation?"

James nodded, embarrassed. "That conversation."

Al pressed his lips together tightly, to stop himself laughing. "James Cape, did you just proposition me?"

James raised two fingers at him. "Fuck off, Al." He leaned his head back against his bedroom wall with a *thunk*. "Seriously, though, I'm getting desperate."

Al rolled his eyes. "You do know how to flatter a guy, don't you? Nice to know I'm your first stop for desperation."

"Oh, you weren't," James assured him. "I tried another one-night stand—can't think how you put up with doing it all the time; it was horrible. You're the last resort."

"Thanks," Al said dryly.

He was sitting cross-legged at the end of James's bed, just as he'd done times out of mind in the last ten years. It was weird looking across at him, discussing having sex with him. They'd discussed sex a million and one times in a million and one ways, but not about doing it with each other. At least, except for that other time where Al had offered to sleep with James. James hadn't thought, even then, that he'd ever take him up on the offer. And yet here he was, looking at Al quite seriously and discussing fucking him. It was surreal.

"Did you mean it, though?" James asked. "It won't make things weird, will it?"

"Yes, I meant it—and no, it won't," Al said simply. "Okay, let's go through it bit by bit. James, you're pretty good-looking, so it's not exactly going to be a hardship for me. What's more, if it got weird every time I slept with someone, I'd have to emigrate pretty soon because there would be no one left for normality. I have designs on your virtue but none at all on your heart; but if you start being weird with me, I'll slap you to the far side of tomorrow, because you're my best mate, and you ought to know better. And I'm here all summer, so we can literally try the best-friends-with-benefits thing. As long as you're not fussed by my sleeping around—and yes, I always use protection, as you well bloody know since you've been asking personal questions of that nature for years—it should be fine."

"How can you make something weird sound so very not weird?" James asked, smiling at his best friend.

"It's just sex, James," Al said, shaking his head. "It's fun. That's all. Now, if we're agreed on all that, and you're serious about it, are you going to actually snog me, or are you just going to talk my ear off? Because nice though the conversation is, if we're really going to do this, I'm ready for a bit more."

"Kissing," James said thoughtfully.

"To start with, I thought?" Al said politely. "Rather than just ripping all our clothes off and you sticking your cock where the sun doesn't shine without any buildup? I presume you're still all with the 'waiting for Laurie' thing, incidentally, as far as being fucked goes?"

James blushed. "It's not like that. Not exactly...not any more. He's never going to be interested, is he? But yeah, still. When I've done it at uni, I've always...you know."

"I reckoned you probably would," Al said, nodding. "Still, I thought maybe not actual—you know, fucking, right now. Start a bit slowly, if you get my drift? Don't want to frighten you with my expertise," he added, grinning.

"I appreciate your concern. Idiot. But that sounds good," James finished, more seriously.

"Come here, then." But Al belied his words by scrambling across the bed so he was sitting next to James.

They looked at each other for a second, and then Al moved his head towards James's. Just as their lips touched, however, there was the sound of footsteps on the stairs and then the voice of Gillie, James's mother.

"Hey, boys," she called cheerfully. "Can I come in a second?"

James pulled away from Al as if he'd been shot. Al collapsed into giggles.

"Of course, Mum," James said, trying to look as if he hadn't been just about to snog his best friend.

Gillie poked a messy auburn head round the door and smiled at them both. "Sorry. Just to let you know, Terry and I are off now to this bloody awful party to say goodbye to his workmates. Won't be back till gone midnight, I shouldn't think. Have fun. You'll have more fun than us, I'm sure." She looked teasingly at Al. "No wild parties, Al."

Al sighed, grinning engagingly at Gillie. "Not even a little one?" he wheedled.

Gillie laughed. "Not even a little one. See you tomorrow. I'm glad you're staying here this summer. It doesn't seem like a proper house without both my sons here."

"You can't get rid of me that easily," Al assured her.

"Bye, Mum. Hope it's not as awful as you think. Drink lots," James advised.

"Yes, do. You're funny when you're drunk," Al agreed helpfully.

Gillie shook her head at the pair of them. "Some of us are not twenty years old. Hangovers last longer at our advanced ages, you know. See you in the morning, loves." She came in properly, swiped a kiss at each of their heads, and vanished with a wave of her hand.

When she was gone, Al and James's eyes met, Al's full of laughter.

"Well. That could've been embarrassing," James commented, pressing his hands to his face.

Al couldn't control the giggles which had been bubbling under the surface the entire time. "God, Jamie, you're such a perv. I nearly died when she called me her son. Not only have you been fantasising about fucking one of your mum's best friends for years, you're about to have sex with her adopted kid. You're utterly screwed, mate."

"Shut up!" James heard the front door slam and the car start up as he pushed Al over onto his back on the bed and put an arm to his throat. "You're such a wanker."

Al fought back; they'd been horsing around like this since they were kids, and it came almost as naturally as breathing. James was the larger and stronger, but Al fought dirty, always had. An elbow to James's stomach had him gasping for breath, and before he could recover himself, he was underneath, and Al was on top.

"Thought it was you who was the wanker," Al murmured, grinning down at him. "Thought that was what you wanted me to help with."

"I..."

James didn't get any further than that because Al kissed him.

And it *was* a kiss. There was no playing about in the way Al kissed. None of the earlier teasing; nothing tentative or uncertain about it. Lips firm and warm against James's. Mouth opening against his, tongue exploring with practised ease. A hand in James's hair; a slender, lithe body pressing against James's. Al had been right; he was very good at this indeed. Instead of fighting, James found his arms going around Al, his own tongue responding to Al's sensual assault of his mouth. They kissed, and kissed; and when Al broke away, James found that he was very short of breath...and very, very hard.

"Fuck," he mumbled.

Al was looking down at him with slightly dazed eyes. "Bloody hell, Jamie, you're good at that," he said. He shifted his body against James's, and James realised that he wasn't the only one sporting an erection. "How did I not know you'd be so good?"

"Oh, right," James retorted, trying to keep his tone light and his brain unscrambled, "like you're supposed to know by sight whether someone's a good kisser or not."

It had felt good—really good—when Al had moved against him. James did the same, pressing up against his friend, just a little bit.

"God, like that," Al agreed, responding back again. A smile quirked the corner of his mouth. "And, of course, I know these things usually. You probably just put me off by being such a tosser most of the time that I never really thought about it."

"Mm."

James couldn't be bothered to argue. It felt too good lying here like this. He tugged Al's head down and kissed him again, continuing to frot against him as he did so. Al's response, if possible, was more passionate even than before—he seemed to be trying to consume James—until James was close to moaning into his mouth.

"Fuck, James," Al said breathlessly, tearing himself away a second time with some reluctance, "if we carry on like this, I'll come in my pants. Haven't done that since I was seventeen. Fuck."

He rolled off James and lay beside him, his hand going out to stroke James's cock through his trousers, one leg still thrown over James's, his own erection digging into James's hip. They rested there together for a few seconds, just touching gently. Al's hand slowed on James's cock and then just laid there across it. James had one arm underneath Al, holding him in against his side. It should have been peculiar, but maybe James was still too distracted to think about it. Neither of them had come, yet—James was pretty sure that would change before the end of the evening—but it was as if they both needed a break from the unexpected intensity of what had happened between them.

"So..." James said, at last.

"Yeah," agreed Al.

"Um."

"Think it will help?" Al asked, his tone brisk and cheerful.

James lay his head back on the pillow and shut his eyes for a second. "Yes. I think it will help." He opened them again. "Thanks, Al."

"My pleasure." Al grinned. "Quite literally."

"It was..."

"Yes."

"Is it always like that, for you?"

"No."

"Oh."

James pondered this. He'd had very enjoyable sex in the past; had thought he knew pretty much all he needed to know, in fact. But he and Al hadn't even fucked yet—hell, they hadn't even touched each other's naked bodies—and this was still better than anything he'd ever experienced before, even with Fred. It hadn't been idle boasting when Al had said he was good. Yet Al, too, had felt something. James had wondered whether it was just his comparative lack of experience, but apparently there was more to it than that.

"Food?" suggested Al in a hopeful tone of voice. "We could maybe do with a bit of a break, stop thinking so much. Plus—food."

"You're always bloody hungry," James said, but he was not loath to agree. It had been rather more of an experience than he'd been anticipating, considering it was with Al. He swung his legs off the bed. "Come on then."

"I don't eat properly during term time," Al informed him. "It's terribly sad."

"Tragic," James agreed. "Try it on Mum; it doesn't work on me."

It did, though, in truth. Privately, James was worried that Al actually didn't eat properly at university. From what Al was saying, between the time he was dedicating to his studies—quite a lot, because when Al was interested in something, he was really interested in something—and the time he was dedicating to drinking and sleeping around, James wasn't sure he could possibly ever have a moment to eat. Plus he was one of the worst cooks James had ever known. James, on the other hand, loved cooking and was popular in his student house for that as much as anything else—if anyone was going to pull together a big pot of chilli for ten students, or five different curries to suit five different tastes, it was James. He cooked, the others washed up, and everyone was happy. Games evenings on a Friday night, with lots of wine and a mountain of food cooked by James, had become standard in the Rainbow House—because despite all of the attempts to avoid it, Jenny's name had indeed stuck—and were the highlight of week for quite a number of people, from what James had heard said.

So James pottered downstairs to the kitchen and flung a few ingredients about as Al helped himself and James to some wine, which he'd brought back from the shop after his first shift the day before, and before long, there were omelettes with a green salad and a separate tomato and bean salad, and a homemade dressing.

"'S'mazing," Al said appreciatively round a mouthful of omelette.

"It's omelette. I could probably teach even you to cook this," James said dismissively.

Al swallowed hastily and held up his hands in front of him. "No, no, that's absolutely fine, thanks. I'm quite happy to sit here and admire your superlative skill. No cooking lessons required."

James's eyes glinted. "Not even in return for the fucking lessons you seem so certain you're going to give me?"

Al chuckled. "Not so sure about that after the way you kiss. Maybe you're going to be teaching me that, too. Where'd you learn to kiss like that, Jamie?"

"You started it," James said. "I was just along for the ride."

"We'll put it down to my brilliance if you insist," Al agreed insouciantly. "Incidentally, though, if the way to a man's heart is through his stomach, I might end up falling for you. Just a warning."

"I'll take that risk," James assured him. "I think I'm probably safe, what with the—how many people have you slept with this term?"

"Not sure. Do you really want me to count 'em?" Al asked. "Names, details? How much info do you want? Well, I've said it once before this evening, and I'll say it again, you're a perv, James Cape. As to the ones I've slept with more than once, though, that's a bit simpler. Not so many of them."

James shook his head. "Dear, dear, and I thought you were good. You put most of them off at the first try? Very sad."

"I expect that's it." Al nodded, leaning back lazily in his chair and tipping wine into his mouth. If James had been hoping to make Al rise to the bait, he was out of luck. "Anyway, four—and two of them were female. Fun, though, all of it. You?"

"One, as you bloody well know, and it was pretty underwhelming," James retorted.

"Sounds like we're as crap as each other, in that case," Al said. "Good job we've got each other to practise on, eh?"

They finished the meal and retreated to the bedroom after Al washed up, taking the rest of the bottle of wine with them.

"So," said James, looking dubiously at Al and finishing the wine in his glass, "what now?"

"Bloody hell, if that's a sample of your chat-up lines, no wonder you don't get far."

"I don't want to get far, you tosser."

"I'm teasing. Come here." Al reached out an arm for James and dragged him close. "Kissing. Kissing was good, remember? We might add in some touching this time for good measure."

"Bloody difficult to kiss someone without touching them," James grumbled, but his heart wasn't in it.

"Shh," said Al, putting a hand to James's face and turning it to face him. "Kiss me."

So James did. It was better this time even than last time, because he knew what to expect. Knew the direction Al would turn his head, the way Al's hand would sneak behind him to pull him closer. Then Al's other hand landed on his thigh, warm and firm, stroking up towards his groin in little motions. James pulled Al right into his lap so that Al was straddling him, and their mouths were hot and wet against each other's. Al moved his head away and nuzzled round the side of James's neck, pressing biting kisses along his jawbone and down into the soft flesh. He rocked against James for a bit until they were both hard and panting.

"Too many clothes," Al panted, pulling away and stripping off his trousers and pants.

James followed suit and took off Al's top for good measure, wanting to run his hands over Al's chest, which was surprisingly muscular. Al was, James realised, really an extremely hot bloke.

He probably should have noticed this before, but Al had always just been Al—James's best mate. Still, this was not an inopportune moment to realise how much he actually fancied the guy he was snogging, James supposed, even if it was a bit peculiar when that guy happened to be Al Hitchins. Al went back to straddling him, and without the trousers, it was better than anything that had happened between them before. James's cock rubbed up against Al's, pushing between their stomachs, and Al groaned and reached down between them, taking them both in his grasp.

"Fuck, Al."

The feeling of Al's hand working both their cocks was too good. James had an awful feeling he was going to start moaning or something, which would be horrendously embarrassing. Maybe fucking around with his best friend was not such a good plan. James wasn't sure how much control he was supposed to have, but it felt as if he was in the process of losing every single last bit of it; and how was he supposed to face Al again after Al had reduced him to a quivering mass of nerves, and they both knew it?

Except that it was Al whose breathing was heavy; Al who was murmuring, "James, god, so good, Jamie, oh god, fuck, *fuck*;" and fucking up into his own hand and against James's cock with completely shameless abandon, apparently having no such worries about afterwards or what he might look like. James stopped worrying, giving himself up to the sensation and rutting against Al, his mouth busy on any part of Al's skin he could find, his fingers roaming all over Al's back and down to his arse. He cupped Al's buttocks, pulling him tighter still against him, and Al groaned loudly, his head falling onto James's shoulder as he cried "Jamie" and came.

The feeling of Al's come against his skin sent James shuddering over into his own orgasm, his hands clenching and unclenching against Al's back as it overtook him. His blood pulsed in his ears, and Al's sweat flavoured his tongue where his mouth was open against his neck. He felt terrible and wonderful all at once, his head spinning.

"God," said Al, his head still resting heavily on James's shoulder, a few minutes later. "Yes, so. Something like that."

"Apparently so," said James, chasing bravely for his scattered wits.

"Mm, well." Al peeled himself off James, running a hand over himself thoughtfully, as if to see the state he was in. Which, in fact, well might have been the intention. "Thanks for that."

"I think that's supposed to be my line," James said. "You're the one doing me a favour."

Al snorted. "Yeah, it was bloody awful for me, as you noticed," he said. "Okay if I bags the shower now?"

"Fine."

James watched, amused, as Al wandered off to the bathroom. It seemed Al had been right—there was no room for embarrassment where he was concerned. James had just had sex with his best friend, with no intention of there ever being any sort of romantic relationship between them, and it was completely a non-issue as far as Al was concerned. And, frankly, James was feeling considerably better about the world right now. Possibly Al was on to something—sex was, in fact, just sex. A physical pleasure. But James hadn't always found it so. He suspected he needed some sort of emotional element in order to enjoy sex, but it turned out that friendship would do for that. There was, in fact, a great relief in knowing that Al had no expectations of him except that their friendship would continue from precisely where it had been before they...well, before they'd just come in a big sweaty heap. Al strolled back in, dressed in a towel, and gave James an appreciative look.

"You look very sexy all sweaty and covered in come, with that T-shirt sticking to you," he commented. "Nice look. Suits you."

"Thanks. I'm still getting in the shower."

"Good idea. I just nabbed the last towel, though, so you'd better get some more out, otherwise Gillie'll do her nut when she gets home."

Gillie's son had just had sex with her adopted son, but Al was worried about towels. Well, there was something for perspective.

"I'm onto it," he assured Al, making an effort to search through the cupboard for some appropriate-sized towels for the bathroom. There wasn't too much of a problem—Gillie and Terry had their own en suite. James's dad needed a specially adapted shower in order that he could get in and out of it by himself—but James's mum always wanted there to be towels available in the general use bathroom in case someone came round, which was fair enough. James wasn't quite sure what had happened to the previous hand towel, but that was the sort of thing which was a mystery of life in any household.

Clean and dry—and the bathroom fitted out appropriately with towels—the two young men finished the bottle of wine in companionable spirits.

Chapter Five

THEY HAD PENETRATIVE sex five days later. Al had found a woman to go home with in between—"Yes, James, we used condoms"—and was looking quite cheerful about it. James unexpectedly felt a bit guilty about his own experience with Al in the face of this, and he said so.

Al looked at him in blank bewilderment. "Why on earth?"

"It feels like I'm taking advantage of you," James said, a bit embarrassed. "You know, you've got plenty of people you could be seeing and whatever."

"And I am," Al pointed out. "I was, in fact. Sarah. Lovely girl. Butterfly tattoo on her shoulder—a bit unoriginal, but it was nicely done, and it suited her. She was a bit like a butterfly, really, all sort of fluttery in bed. It was good." He gave James a bit of a grin. "Not as good as you, Jamie, obviously, but not bad. She's down with some mates, so we had a hotel room to go back to, and she's back up North tomorrow, so no hard feelings about parting."

"Yeah, but—"

"Overthinking," said Al in a sing-song voice, shutting James up effectively by blocking his mouth with his own. "Also," he added, when James was quite distracted from his earlier thoughts, "it's about time you fucked me. Talk about taking advantage—here I am positively begging you to take advantage of me, and I'm still waiting."

James looked down at Al, a glint in his eye. "Okay, if *that's* the way you feel about it, I can probably do something about that."

"Encouraging," Al said, his arms wrapped round James's shoulders.

James picked him up and carried him over to the bed. "Bloody hell, you're heavier than you look," he commented, panting a little as he dropped him.

"Wuss."

"I'll tell Mum to stop feeding you."

"Oh yeah? Going to tell her why?" Al gibed.

"Shut up."

"Make me."

"I will."

James did. Just as Al had prevented him sharing any more of his 'overthinking', James stopped Al's digs by kissing him hard and firm. Al had no complaints, dragging James down onto the bed and arching up into him in such a way that it wasn't long before James had forgotten what they'd been arguing about; had forgotten everything, in fact, save the fact that Al had asked him to fuck him, and James was prepared to do just that.

"How much prep do you need?" James asked, dragging Al's clothes off piece by piece, followed by his own trousers and pants.

"Well," Al drawled, "I don't have much sex, you know."

"Eff off. It'd serve you right if I just fucked straight into you."

"It would, of course," Al agreed, tangling his legs around James's as he efficiently undid the buttons on James's shirt—the only thing left either of them was wearing. Apparently Al was not prepared to be the only one totally naked tonight. "But you're not going to."

James heaved a sigh. "No, of course I'm not, you wanker. But still."

"Am I prepared to have unprotected sex with you?" Al asked provocatively, pushing the shirt over James's shoulders. "I don't know where you've been."

Coming from anyone, it would have been impolite. Coming from Al, it was incendiary.

"You are"—James leaned over to haul the lube and a foil-packaged condom out of his drawer, and waving the latter at his best friend with a roll of his eyes—"the most"—he unwrapped the condom, rolling it down over his heavy, hard cock—"bloody annoying fuck ever. Happy now?" He lubed his sheathed cock liberally as Al willingly spread his legs, and then shoved two sticky fingers inside Al. It was much harder than he'd ever have considered doing to anyone else, but Al just made a little noise as James pushed his fingers into him, then a longer, more satisfied one.

"Like that," Al said, on a hissed-out breath.

"Oh yeah?"

James was careful but determined. He moved the fingers to and fro for a short while, but not too long. Much more quickly than he'd done on previous occasions, he exchanged them for his cock, and entered Al slowly, but without the pauses he might have left with another partner. Al didn't seem to care.

"Oh yeah," he agreed, pushing back up against James. "God, Jamie, fuck me."

Suddenly James realised how Al got so many partners. He had no inhibitions, no fears about saying or showing what he wanted. James and all his previous lovers had had an edge of caution, of trying to do the right thing or make it right for the other person; of worrying about whether this way or that was better, what the other person might be thinking of them. With Al, it was instinctual. He wasn't selfish—even as he encouraged James on with words, his hands were touching James's body, turning him on by means that James hadn't even known existed before tonight. James's pleasure was as important to him—perhaps more—than his own. But he knew what he was doing; he knew what he wanted, he knew what James wanted, and he knew how to get it. Perhaps he didn't even know how he knew. Perhaps he didn't even know he knew. It didn't matter. James still felt, somewhere deep inside him, that if you loved someone, it could be even better than this. It could hit heights nothing else could reach. But without that? There could be no one with whom he could enjoy sex—enjoy! Such a pathetic word for the feeling!—more than Al.

James leaned down and kissed Al, his lips opening against his friend's. He pushed his tongue into Al's mouth in much the same way he'd pushed his cock into Al's arse; and Al responded in a similar way, welcoming him in. Encouraging him. Pressing against him and making small noises of contentment which flowed right through James. James fucked him with his tongue, flicking it in and out of Al's mouth, tasting every bit of Al until Al was moaning and thrusting his hips up against James's, fucking himself on James's cock. Then James started to move—long, slow strokes which changed the tenor of Al's moans to a lower pitch. James's own breathing was hitching and catching; he couldn't continue the steady pace, instead moving faster as he watched Al's movements, the way Al's body shone with sweat and his eyes glazed as he reached down to touch himself, wrapping his hand around his own cock and stroking himself in time with James's thrusts.

Their orgasms were almost simultaneous—James didn't know, afterwards, which of them had come first; he had been too bound up, he admitted to himself, in the feelings of his own body to worry about Al's at just that moment. But when they collapsed, panting, it was clear that Al had come too. There was a flush of pink on his usually pale cheeks, which spread down his chest in a fascinating fashion, and his breathing was still wavering and heavy as he blinked slowly at James. They lay together for a bit, but clearly Al was not one for cuddling; he pulled away, wriggling into his own space on the bed.

"You take up too much bloody room," he complained.

"I'm twice your size." James peeled the condom off carefully and winced at the stickiness it left in its wake.

"Now that's just showing off," Al said, a slow smile emerging on his face.

"Oh, shut up." James rolled his eyes. Al could make anything into innuendo; and although he was, in fact, slightly bigger in that department than Al, there was not a lot in it. "So. Do you feel sufficiently taken advantage of?"

The smile grew. "For the moment, Jamie. For the moment. Not bad. You'll definitely have to practise, though."

"Wanker."

"Don't need to be." Al lay back, spreading his limbs over far too much of the bed for his size. "'Feel free to take advantage of me anytime' is the basic message."

James, deciding that if Al could play it cool so could he, swung his legs off the bed and hoped they could still carry him without trembling. "Fine," he said, standing up with only the slightest hesitation. "But this is my bed, and you've got your own. I'm heading for the bathroom, and I want you out by the time I get back."

"A bully as well." Al shut his eyes. "Be gone to your shower, Jamie-boy. I'll leave you in peace. I am, as you said, sufficiently taken advantage of for one night, at any rate."

THUS BEGAN WHAT was, in some ways, the longest relationship James had ever had. It *wasn't* a 'relationship', of course—Al was quite clear about that. Since he'd left school, he'd made a firm policy never to get romantically involved with anyone, and he had kept to it. Not that James was the least interested in romance with Al. The thought, quite honestly, was just peculiar. But Al had also discovered that there were plenty of people at the uni who were happy to have no-strings sex, so he had at least three long-term fuck-buddies, as he cheerfully termed them, whom he'd been seeing for most of the year, if not longer. There were, as well, always people to pick up for a night or so and Al was, it seemed, an expert at that, too. James was just another enjoyable partner, which suited them both very well. Al admitted to James, however, that he was finding it rather more difficult now that it was the summer—he didn't feel it was appropriate to bring casual partners back to the Capes' house, and his longer-term partners had all gone home for the summer holidays. So Al was currently reliant on whoever he wanted to shag as a one-off having accommodation of their own... "Or at least a car," he added as an afterthought.

"Good job you've got me at home, then," James retorted. "A sex-starved Al would be a horror to behold."

Al responded with something impossibly vulgar, and James twisted his arm behind his back, at which point Gillie came into the room.

"Still fighting in the sitting room, boys? Seriously?" she teased. "Please don't break the television."

They laughed—she'd been saying that to James and Al since they were rowdy ten-year-olds.

"Bless Gillie"—Al murmured as she left the room again—"she never comes in at the really interesting moments, does she?"

"Thank fuck for that," James said fervently. "She's my actual mother, you know. There are some things she doesn't need to hear about."

Al glanced over at him—James had let go of his arm by this point. "Better hope she hasn't been talking to Laurie, then," he said.

James grimaced. "She promised not to. She knew something was up before I left for uni, but she promised she'd leave well alone. Anyway, it's nearly two years ago. Old news now."

"To everyone but you," Al said softly, his eyes full of sympathy.

James huffed a breath. "Yeah. To everyone but me."

However, he bumped into Laurie early on in the summer. Although they'd managed to get over the worst of their awkwardness the first Christmas after the rejection, they had usually got by with brief superficial conversations and not much else. But things seemed to have changed suddenly this summer. James wasn't quite sure why, but they found themselves getting on better than ever, and unexpectedly, Laurie invited James to go out for a drink with him one evening.

"Thanks," said James, surprised but not unwilling. It still hurt to be around Laurie, knowing that Laurie had no feelings for him but mild friendship, but he liked Laurie's company and half a loaf, after all, was better than no bread.

"Glad you came," Laurie commented when they met, a pint in front of each of them. "Al's bloody cold to me when he sees me around. I wondered if you were feeling the same way."

"Don't be ridiculous—Al's never cold to anyone," James said, taking a swig of beer.

"Oh yeah?" Laurie looked disbelieving. "I took one of his seminars last term when the usual lecturer was off sick, and there was a question about the motivation of one of the characters in a film, who had spent most of his time on-screen shooting various people. Al looked me in the eye and told me that some people were quite capable of being tossers without any motivation to it at all. I took the hint."

James spluttered with laughter. "Sorry," he said apologetically. "Oh, Al. But he's been saying things like that to you for years; you know he has."

Laurie laughed in turn. "Generally not in public. Fortunately, I don't think any of the other students picked up on anything other than Al being more than usually Al-ish, though. Still, out of a matter of interest, what *did* I do to him?"

James was silent. If Laurie really didn't know, James wasn't going to tell him. If he did, it was a stupid sort of question to be putting to James. Al was, after all, very, very loyal. If James was still upset by Laurie—which he undeniably was, present truce notwithstanding—Al was not going to forgive him easily. He had, in fact, told James what an idiot he was for agreeing to meet with Laurie earlier that evening.

"Knifes twisting in wounds," Al had said darkly.

James had given him a shove. "Shouldn't it be knives? And anyway, you're standing me up for Fenella at the wine shop—"

"She's told me to call her Fen," Al put in smugly. He was enjoying his summer job—alcohol and people, it turned out, were just Al's sort of combination.

"So you can't complain if I go out with someone else."

"Hellfire, James, go out with who the heck you please. You're still an idiot if that person happens to be Laurie," his friend had said.

So silence was really the only option in response to Laurie's question. Laurie appeared to realise this and changed the subject abruptly.

"You're looking happy, anyway. Your mum reckons you're seeing someone. Are you?"

"No, I..." James began automatically. Then he stopped, wondering whether this had been behind Laurie's sudden willingness to spend time with him again. "Yes," he said slowly, "I suppose I am."

It wasn't as if Laurie was about to turn round and declare undying love for him, after all. If Laurie did have any suspicions that James's feelings hadn't changed—though surely after nearly two years, he would have presumed it had worn off—telling him that he was seeing someone else should dampen those down nicely. And it wasn't an entire lie, if by 'seeing' one meant 'fucking'. He and Al were having sex on an extremely regular basis, and it was bloody good. Essentially meaningless, emotionally, but bloody good nonetheless.

Fuck it. Why couldn't Laurie just have wanted him back? James shook his head to rid himself of the unwanted thoughts. This was not the moment for rehashing his and Laurie's past history. He smiled insincerely at Laurie.

"Congratulations," Laurie said.

James shrugged. "It's nothing serious."

"Now you're beginning to sound like Al," Laurie teased.

"Maybe I've taken a leaf out of his book," James said, looking sideways at Laurie.

But Laurie shook his head. "Not you. You're not like that."

"Maybe I wasn't once, but people change," James said. "What about you?"

"Stubbornly single," Laurie said cheerfully. "Stubbornly single. Not even an Al-like liaison in my near past, and it's not looking like one in my near future, either. Still, when I don't have Al giving me grief, I'm enjoying the teaching. And they're suggesting there might be a proper lectureship—not a sessional one—going in the near future. Mind you, the last person they said that to ended up out of a job altogether, so I'm not banking on it."

"Is that what you want to do?" James asked, curious.

Laurie looked at him seriously. "More than anything. The research assistant job is interesting, but people are more so. Watching them change, develop their opinions as they go through. I'd like to be able to help them do that, give them pointers in the right direction. Some of them have so little confidence, and with a bit of encouragement, they suddenly realise they can do this—just because it's not school doesn't mean it's beyond them. I've met a couple of students, the first people in their family ever to go to university, and they were both convinced they were set to fail, but they're doing just fine. Whereas others—they come in thinking they're the best thing ever, and then they meet university work and realise it's not all partying and drinking and just turning up every now and again, and it all falls apart." He took a gulp of his beer. "To be honest, I wondered if Al would be like that."

James shook his head. "You don't know him as well as you think you do."

"Clearly I don't. Not," Laurie added, "that he isn't making a name for himself with the drinking et cetera—mostly the et cetera. But Annabel—she's the professor who supervised my thesis; she's great—says he's also one of the best students she's got. Don't you dare tell him that, mind."

James laughed at that. "Laurie, do you seriously think he doesn't know? You look at the outside of Al and you forget what he's like when he's really into something. Think about when he was younger and it was the Marvel comics—he's loving the films of those, by the way. If he cares about something, he really cares. And he really cares about this course."

"Apparently so." Laurie looked sad. "I wonder who else I'm misjudging."

Me, James wanted to say. *Me. You look at me and you see a kid. Why can't you see any further than that? I'd be good for you.* Instead, he said, "Most people tend to see Al wrong. We're used to it."

"You speak as though you're one person—you and him—sometimes."

"Sometimes I think we might as well be," James confessed. "I don't know who I'd be without Al. He's been part of my life for so long."

"You're lucky."

"You have Mum," James pointed out.

"Yes. Gillie's pretty special," Laurie said. "But I was nineteen before I got to know her. You've known Al how long?"

"Since we were nine or so. Best friends since ten. You'd think he'd be sick of me by now," James said lightly.

"No," Laurie said quietly. "No, I wouldn't think that."

There was silence for a moment. James drank more beer to cover his confusion. He felt like something had been said that he hadn't heard, somehow. That some message should have been conveyed which he hadn't got. But then, maybe it was just because this was Laurie, and James was always looking for more in every interaction between them.

"But your work's going well," James said, getting them back on safer territory.

It was Laurie's turn to drink. "Yes. Very well."

Looking back on it, James wasn't sure whether to count the evening a success or not. On the whole, he reckoned it had been; he hadn't embarrassed himself in front of Laurie, nor had they fought. At the same time, there was always a sense of frustration, of something missing. Something that there could have been between them but wasn't. He tried to say some of this to Al when he got home, but Al was unsympathetic.

"Like I said, you were an idiot to go out with him. In a not-going-out-with-him sense, that is," he said flatly.

"Thanks for your support," James retorted. He hesitated. "If you must know, I've agreed to meet up with him again."

"Then you're a fucking twit." For once in his life, Al hunched a grumpy shoulder towards James and walked off to his own room without saying anything more.

But Al was repentant in the morning.

"Jamie, I'm sorry." Al barged into James's bedroom at an hour where James would really have rather liked still to be asleep.

"Huh?" said James, stupidly, trying to crack his eyes open and wondering why he was bothering.

Al sat down heavily on his legs, and James grunted. "About last night. I was an arse. I'm sorry."

"S'all right," James said groggily. "Can you get off my legs now?"

"Sorry." Al moved so that he was sitting next to, rather than on, James. "I don't get this love thing, Jamie. I dunno. It seems to make people act like utter dicks."

"*You* can manage that without love," James said, rubbing his face ruefully and putting up with being thoroughly awakened.

"Thanks for that," Al said ironically. "Guess I deserve that one. Anyway, if you want to keep seeing Laurie and rubbing your own nose in it, go for it. I'll listen and do my best to say the right sympathetic things, okay?"

"Okay. Can I go back to sleep now?" James asked politely.

Al sighed. "Oh, fuck you, James."

"Not right now, thanks." James closed his eyes again and turned over in bed.

When he next opened them, Al was gone.

Chapter Six

BUT JAMES CONTINUED to see Laurie a couple of times a week for a drink, and he had to admit that he enjoyed every minute of it. Or nearly every minute. Occasionally, it was undeniable, Laurie would say something so clueless that James would have to pretend to be very busy drinking his beer, or listening to the music, or even excuse himself to go to the toilet and swear quietly in peace. But in general, Laurie was great company, making James laugh more than he'd done for ages, and sharing insights with him which warmed James through in a way he tried not to think about.

They had just sunk their third pints on a more than usually drunken evening, when Laurie said casually, "So, final year coming up, then. Thought at all about what you want to do afterwards?"

James flushed. He'd talked to Al about his ideas and mentioned them a bit to his parents, but he was still shy about it. The composing, he was sure no one would take seriously—though Al had, in fact, been much more interested than James had expected. "Cool," Al had said. "When I'm directing films, you can write the music." James had laughed at him for this flight of fancy but he'd appreciated the support, nonetheless. But the teaching...well, that was awkward in a whole new way. James had never thought of himself as a teacher, and he hadn't been a particularly enthusiastic student in his school days, though he'd been fortunate enough to be academically gifted nonetheless. His grades had been good, even if his attitude had not always been complimented by his teachers. The thought of teaching in schools themselves was horrific still; but the thought of one-on-one tutoring, showing people how the guitar worked and what a variety of things one could do with it... That definitely appealed. The idea of Laurie dismissing him—or worse, laughing at him— was hard to take.

"I guess," he mumbled, staring into his fourth beer.

"Don't tell me, will you?" Laurie said, gently teasing. "Is it that bad? Are you taking up organised crime?"

James grinned. "No, I'll leave that to Al. He'd be a natural." They laughed, and then James said awkwardly, "I just...don't want you to think I'm an idiot."

Laurie's blue eyes could be very soft on occasion. "I won't think that."

"Well." James swallowed. "I'm, kind of...thinking about teaching. Not," he added hastily, "like classrooms and stuff. Just...guitar."

"Why on earth would I think that's idiotic?"

James shrugged. "The world's probably full of guitar teachers. They don't need someone like me messing around, putting people off the instrument forever."

"Is that what Al said?" Laurie asked sharply.

James, halfway through a mouthful of beer, choked. "No. Why would you think that?"

"It just sounded...a bit Al-ish, is all."

"No. He did say that he couldn't think of anything worse than teaching incompetents to do something I did well," James said, "but if it seemed like a good idea to me, good on me. He wouldn't cut me down like that, you know. Not if it mattered to me." He was aware he sounded slightly defensive and was annoyed with himself for it, but sometimes Laurie seemed to have it in for Al.

"I'm sorry," Laurie said. "I didn't mean to offend you. Or insult Al. It's just—why would you think I'd say something like that, or even consider it?"

Because that's what I've been thinking. And because I'd hate most of all to hear you say it because what you think matters too much, even now. But James didn't say that aloud. He just looked back at his beer as if it was the most fascinating thing he'd ever seen.

"Dunno. It's just, it seemed like a weird thing to want to do, is all."

"Well, Gillie's a bloody good lecturer, and you're her son," Laurie pointed out. "God knows whether teaching is genetic, but if it is, you've inherited some good genes. How would you go about it?"

"Get a qualification after I finish my degree? Look for jobs like anybody else. I just want to teach single students, give them the basics. Maybe a bit more, if they want it. But it'd be nice to have a proper qualification. If I am going to do it, I want to do it right."

"And what put it in your head? Sorry, am I asking too many questions?" Laurie apologised. "But it sounds brilliant, and you'd be great at it. I just...never knew you were thinking that way."

"Girl at uni wanted me to show her how to play," James said briefly. "She said she'd pay me, so we gave it a go. I teach her stuff; she buys me a drink and occasionally some chips. And...and, well, I like it. And she does, too. She's getting quite good. Told her she'll be better than me soon."

"You charmer, you." Laurie smiled. "I bet she fancies you, too."

"Right," said James flatly. "Because she couldn't just like my teaching."

"I didn't mean it like that," Laurie said, sighing. "Sorry. I seem to be putting my foot in it this evening. But I can imagine you being good at teaching. You've got the patience. And you're good at making people feel important to you."

James tried not to stare at Laurie. What the fuck did he mean by that?

"Erm, thanks? I guess?"

"I was going to say 'It was meant as a compliment' but it wasn't. It was meant as the truth," Laurie said simply. "I think you'd be good at teaching. Maybe especially people who are lacking in self-confidence—a few lessons with you and they'd start feeling like they could do anything they wanted to."

James processed this for a few seconds and then realised he was blushing. Had Laurie really just said…? Laurie was drinking his beer as if he'd said nothing unusual, and James gave himself an internal shake. Laurie was just being nice. They were both silent, and then Laurie spoke again.

"I'm sorry about earlier. What I said about Al. I didn't mean to cast aspersions on him; it's just that it's the sort of thing he says to me, that's all, and—"

"Oh." Yes, James supposed it was. That *did* make some sense, actually—Laurie hadn't been being unkind about Al for no good reason, which was reassuring. "Sorry," he said, not sure whether he was apologising for himself or Al.

"It doesn't bother me." Laurie smiled. "I'm used to it by now. It's just, you looked…hurt, and I just…I worry."

He reached out and touched James's upper arm with large warm fingers. James had nearly finished his fourth pint, and Laurie's fingers were on his arm, and he was smiling at him, and it was all too much. He hadn't realised he'd leaned across until suddenly his thigh was pushed up against Laurie's on the pub bench; his hand on Laurie's shoulder; his mouth seeking out Laurie's own. Laurie tasted of beer and warmth, and oh god, this was—

This was Laurie almost falling off the far side of the bench in his attempt to get away.

"Um... No, no, James. No. Bad plan." Laurie detached himself from James with more haste than tact. "You're involved with someone, remember? You've got a boyfriend—who is not me."

"Told you. Not that involved," James said, not backing off. "Al-like lee...lise...lisamon... Wait, no, not quite right. Y'know."

"James, you're drunk," Laurie said, and although James was, indeed, drunk, he could hear the notes of desperation and panic in Laurie's voice, and it stung. "Look. Come on. It's probably time we were going home anyway."

Laurie stood up, and James, perforce, let go of him. Fuck. He'd messed it up again. Laurie wasn't interested in the slightest. He was backing off with...well, hell, James would say 'indecent' haste were it not for the fact that Laurie was clearly trying to avoid anything even vaguely indecent anywhere in James's vicinity.

"Home," James agreed in a hollow voice.

He followed Laurie out of the pub, stumbling slightly as they got to the doorway, which had a step that James had forgotten. He fell against Laurie, who flinched back as if he'd been hit, which did nothing for James's ego. Fuck. Fuck, why had he been so stupid? Except Laurie had been so damn *nice* to him, and then he'd smiled like that, and touched James's arm; and that had been enough. Enough, apparently, to make James act like a total bloody dickhead. Laurie wasn't interested. When was James going to get that into his thick head? He. Wasn't. Interested. James could wait for decades, and Laurie would still *not be interested in him.* Not in a sexual sense.

"I'll see you home," Laurie said.

"Don't...don't be stoopid," James slurred. "See myself home. Good at that. Done it enough times." *Self-pity. Ni-ice.*

"I'll see you into a taxi," Laurie compromised. He was standing a couple of feet away from James, as if worried that James would jump him again the moment they got within touching distance of each other. It wasn't flattering. James tried to squash down quite how humiliated he felt and concentrate on getting through the next few moments.

"Taxi. Yeah." He checked his pockets. "'S'all right. I have a tenner. Won't be more, will it? Prices haven't gone up that much since I've been away?"

"I'll talk to the driver. It won't be a problem." Laurie sounded relieved to be getting rid of him—desperate, in fact.

James, you're drunk. That detachment, like James was some sort of cockroach clinging to Laurie. James felt sick, and it wasn't the amount of alcohol he'd consumed which was causing it. He wanted to dig a hole and never, ever come out of it. Please, let him never have to see Laurie—his mother's best friend, for fuck's sake; the person he'd been going for a drink with a couple of times a week for the last three weeks—please let him never have to see him again. Like that was going to happen. James laughed bitterly and realised Laurie was giving him a strange look.

"Sorry. Sorry. Drunk," he said unnecessarily. "Beer. It does that." He was wittering. James didn't witter. Except for when he'd already embarrassed himself beyond compare. Apparently his mouth thought things couldn't get any worse. Well, at least, he hadn't told Laurie he loved him this time. Oh great. Well, that made everything all right, James thought sarcastically to himself. Yeah. Fabulous.

"Taxi," Laurie said, with evident relief, and poured James into it. He had a word with the driver and leaned in to say to James, "I've paid him, so nothing to worry about. Get home safely. Take care. Night, James."

James said nothing until the taxi was going. Then, he looked after the retreating figure of Laurie. "Yeah," he said softly. "Night, Laurie."

"AL."

Al groaned and rolled over, looking dopily at James, who was leaning over his bed, shaking him hard by the shoulder. "James? What time is it?"

"8:00 a.m."

"Fuck. Is the house on fire or something?"

"Worse," said James despairingly. He had got approximately two hours sleep the night before, after his second disastrous propositioning of Laurie.

Al yawned and stretched and blinked. "What are you on about?"

James told him.

"Noooo," Al wailed, sitting up suddenly and putting a hand to his face. "Jamie, please tell me this is some kind of early morning practical joke that I'm not awake enough to find amusing."

James, having told the barest details, shook his head, looking at Al with pleading eyes. "What'm I going to do? It's just...he was sitting there being all...all gorgeous, and *Laurie*, and I was quite pissed, so I just leaned across and snogged him, and oh god, oh god, what am I going to do?"

"This," said Al, rubbing a hand over his head, effectively making messy hair considerably messier, "is not something that can be sorted out without coffee. Not at whatever godawful time of day this is." He looked at James. "If you were as pissed as I hope you were to do anything so fucking suicidal, I don't know how you're even conscious."

"Oh, like I've been able to sleep," James retorted. "Just be glad I waited till eight. I've been desperate to talk to you for hours."

"Well, you could at least have made coffee."

"God, you're right." James suddenly realised that in addition to a severe case of mortification and heartbreak, he was also developing a hangover of doom. "My bloody head."

"Serve you damn well right," Al said unsympathetically, grinding the palms of his hands against his face as if forcibly trying to dispel sleep. "Go and make coffee, Jamie, and I'll... God knows. Whatever people do to wake up. Shower. Something."

Ten minutes later, with Al now damp and sleepy, rather than just sleepy, they were sitting on the bed in James's room—always the one for confidences—leaning back against the wall.

"So, what?" Al demanded tersely.

"Argh." James made a determined effort at pulling his own hair out, leaving Al to grab for the coffees, which were in danger of being precipitated to the floor from James's bedside table. James winced at his own abrupt movement, suddenly needing to clutch his head for a second reason. "I don't know. We were— I was talking about this guitar teaching thing, and Laurie was so cool about everything and so nice. Then he smiled at me and— I'd had a few pints and I just—lost it, I guess. Fuck, I don't know. I seriously was quite drunk, and that's all a bit blurry." He shuddered. The next bit—Laurie firmly and humiliatingly turning him down, again—was anything but blurry. James could remember every second of that in technicolour detail. But he wasn't sure he could bear to describe it out loud, even to Al.

"But what made you think it was a good idea in the first place? I thought we'd been through all this."

James sighed, wishing the coffee wasn't quite so hot. He needed it now, not in five minutes' time. "I don't know, exactly. Like I said, I was quite pissed, and we were talking about you, and—"

Al gave an irrepressible snigger. "I'm so good that the very thought of me had you kissing the nearest bloke? Jamie, I'm flattered and all, but—"

"Oh, fuck off." But James didn't even have the energy to make it sound indignant, and Al sobered at once.

"Sorry. Couldn't help myself. A bit like you, apparently," Al added, seemingly unable to help himself once more. "Sorry."

"And he smiled, and he—he touched me—"

"Well, that sounds hopeful," Al said, frowning. "I don't wonder—"

"No, not like that," James interrupted. He sighed. "Just on the arm. But his hands, Al!"

"Laurie does have bloody gorgeous hands," Al admitted disconcertingly. James flicked him a look. "Oh, not like that, you dick. I'm not after him," he said, rolling his eyes. "Just, I can see the appeal. So he touched you, and you—what? Flung yourself at him?"

"Yeah, something like that." James bent his head forward to put it in his hands and was rewarded by an awful thumping inside his skull which made him groan. "Fuck. Fucking hangover. Fuck."

Al passed him a glass of water. "Here. Until the coffee's cool enough to drink. The more liquid you get down yourself, the better. Trust it from the king of morning afters."

"That's not a name to boast about," James mumbled, taking the water and raising his head cautiously to sip from the glass.

"Yeah, and you're in a position to tell me what to boast about, aren't you? So what did he do when you launched your surprise attack?"

"Erm," James said, as if he had to think to remember—as if every fucking second wasn't seared into his brain. "Pretty much fell off the seat, if you must know. Reminded me that I was taken, and—"

"Hang on," Al interrupted. "Taken? What the fuck? Do you mean...? Why's he think that?"

"Oh shit." James had forgotten that he hadn't shared that particular piece of information with Al. "Um, probably because I told him so."

"Something I should know about?" Al asked, eyebrows raised.

"No. No! I was meaning you, you prat. I mean, not that we're— It's just, when we first— Oh fuck it," James said, confusing even himself with his contrasting use of 'we'. "When I first went for a drink with Laurie," he elucidated, "he said Mum reckoned I was seeing someone, and I was going to say I wasn't, but then I thought maybe he'd freak out a bit less about me if I said yes, and because we—you and me, I mean—are..." He trailed off.

"Shagging," Al interposed helpfully, never one to beat about the bush.

"Yeah. So I thought I could say yes, and it wasn't, you know, entirely untrue." James made another attempt at the coffee, which was just about drinkable now. He tried not to shudder at the massive caffeine hit, dreading to think what that would do to his head if he moved that quickly.

"Bloody hell, Jamie, are you totally mad? So you tell him one week you're seeing someone and then try to snog seven bells out of him a couple of weeks later?" Al groaned and shook his head. Even watching the movement made James's head wince in pain. "Well, I suppose it's got one good aspect—he's just going to think you're completely round the twist."

"Yeah." James's insides felt like a lump of lead, and it was not because of the hangover. "He's never going to speak to me again, is he?"

He felt Al stare at him long and hard and wondered whether he looked as rough as he felt. From the expression on Al's face, he probably did. Still, his best friend was never one to give up easily.

"'Course he is," Al said bracingly. "We just need a strategy. Let me think." There was a minute's pause, whilst James investigated a bit more of the inside of his coffee cup, and Al frowned at the duvet cover. Finally, he said, "Okay, okay. We've got this." He took a big gulp of coffee and then winced. "Geez, how strong did you make it?"

"Not strong enough." James didn't think there *was* coffee strong enough for the way he was feeling, all things considered.

"Any stronger and you could use it to fix the roof," Al said pointedly.

"Any weaker and I'd be up there jumping *off* the roof," said James, not entirely joking.

"All right. Back to the point," Al relented. "So you were drunk, okay."

"Yeah, I did kind of notice that." James flinched. "*Am* kind of noticing that," he corrected.

"No, no, no, like—practically paralytic drunk," Al insisted. James opened his mouth to object, but Al hushed him with a gesture. "No, listen to me. You don't remember anything about it, all right?"

"What?"

"It didn't happen. You'd be amazed what didn't happen. Nothing happened. Nothing that you can remember." Al glared at James firmly. "Laurie's not going to mention it. If it's made clear that you have no idea that you made a pass at him at all—"

"How the fuck am I supposed to make that clear without it being clear that I know I did?" James demanded.

"We-ell, you could just act like nothing at all happened," Al offered. "Or I can help you out, if you want?"

"What do you mean?" James asked suspiciously.

"Isn't he supposed to be coming to lunch today?" Al asked.

"Shit." James had forgotten that particular bit of information. Unlike the humiliation of last night, which he would have given years of his life in order actually to forget.

Al grinned. "Leave it to me. Oh, and that hangover you have? It's going to get a lot worse..."

Al was right about the hangover. James didn't have to go to any pretence to need to haunt his bedroom; paracetamol and a darkened room being his closest friends right now. Gillie laughed sympathetically and left him to it. Thus it was that James was safely tucked up in bed when Laurie made his appearance a few hours later.

"Laurie, darling!"

James heard his mother greeting her best friend in her typically enthusiastic way. They were probably hugging, he thought grimly. Laurie didn't mind hugging his mother. It was just James he avoided. But that wasn't fair, he reminded himself. Mum wasn't exactly going to be making a pass at Laurie. An unwanted, drunken, oh-fuck-so-embarrassing-why-did-I-even-do-it pass.

"Hey, Gill. Hi, Terry, Al." A slight pause. Laurie was clearly looking round. "No James?" His voice was a little awkward.

Gillie coughed discreetly. "He's...a little under the weather. It seems he had rather more of a night last night than was good for him. I blame the company he was keeping," she added laughingly.

Laurie mumbled something sheepishly that James couldn't catch. He thought, on the whole, he was probably grateful for it.

"Yeah, what the hell were you and James drinking last night?" James heard Al ask. "I've got to say, you're looking pretty good compared to him. And what did you do with him, anyway? He can't remember a thing after about half past ten. Wandered into my room this morning at some ungodly hour wanting me to make him coffee and asking pathetically if I brought him home because he couldn't remember getting here."

"He never told me that," James's mother said sharply. James winced; he hadn't considered this particular side effect of Al's plan.

"C'mon, Gillie; you must've had nights like that," Al wheedled.

James heard the moment his mother relaxed a little and laughed—Al could usually talk her round—at least to some degree. "If I had, I wouldn't be sharing them with you, Al dear. And I don't imagine James will be wildly appreciative of you giving up his secrets to his mother."

"His father," James's dad added, joining the conversation unexpectedly, "is another matter, of course."

"Ah. Well, of course, I'm not really giving away secrets. I'm making it up as I go along," Al said hastily—and, ironically, truthfully. "He remembers every moment—honest!"

Despite his hangover, James couldn't help a ruefully admiring smile. If anything had been needed to convince Laurie that James certainly did *not* remember anything, it would be Al's apparent attempt to claim that he did. There were advantages of having one of the sneakiest guys in the world as a best friend, he mused.

"Hmm," said Gillie sceptically.

"Ah, dear," said Laurie, this time loud enough to be audible. "Yes, sorry." James could imagine the look he was giving Gillie— the guilty 'please don't hate me for leading your son into bad ways' one. He'd been seeing versions of that since he was twelve and Laurie let him have several sips of his wine one evening—not counting the several more James had taken when Laurie wasn't looking—until Gillie noticed that James was more giggly than usual and demanded the reason why. "I...er...well, I ended up putting him in a taxi and giving the driver directions. He did seem—somewhat drunker than usual, I have to admit."

"Why?" asked Al immediately—just as he would have done if he hadn't known the situation. "Did he do anything wildly embarrassing?"

Thankfully, Al had warned James he was going to pull this line. "There's no way on earth he's going to say that you tried to snog him, mate," he'd promised. "He'll be falling over himself to assure me that you didn't do anything even mildly stupid." Nonetheless, James was glad he'd known in advance. Otherwise, the very question would have sent shivers of horror down his spine. He could still feel his heart thumping in his chest as he waited for Laurie's answer. What if Al had misjudged, and Laurie actually told them? Oh god, he could never face his mother again if that happened. Nor Laurie. Oh god.

"No," said Laurie casually, just as Al had predicted. "Just a little bit slurr-y. You can ask him if he's remembered how to pronounce 'liaison' if you want; he was having a particularly interesting time with the word last night. But I did want to make sure he got home safely."

Despite being upstairs, James blushed about the reminder of the word. He hoped Al wouldn't ask him how it came up. *Al-like liaison* was not a phrase he wanted to be using to his best friend.

"Well, thank heavens for small mercies." His mother's voice again. "I suppose if he's going to get blind drunk with anyone, I'm glad it's you, Laurie."

"Gillie, I'm hurt," Al protested.

Laurie snorted and Gillie and Terry laughed out loud.

"Al, really? Expecting you and James to be good influences on each other is not the way to a long and healthy life!" Gillie teased.

"You'd be amazed," Al murmured, apparently making sure he was directly at the bottom of the stairs so that James could hear him despite the lowered tone. And James had to admit that on this particular occasion Al was saving his bacon in an extremely welcome fashion.

It was still difficult, nonetheless, come lunchtime, when James had promised his mother—and indeed Al, for very different reasons—that he would make an appearance, for James to try to look unconcerned and unembarrassed about the previous night. He settled for the sort of 'mildly embarrassed' which might be covered by having no memory of the evening before.

"Hi, Laurie." He gave a half-smile. "You're looking better than I'm feeling."

"I gathered." There was a slight flush on Laurie's cheeks; he, James realised, was still discomfited by the evening before. Laurie might not think that James could remember it, but that didn't mean that Laurie wouldn't have a crystal clear vision of the way James had— *No, seriously, don't think about that now.*

"Yeah, sorry. Can't remember anything after—I dunno when, to be honest," James lied, hoping his own heating face would be put down to this information.

"James Cape, you should be ashamed of yourself," his mother scolded. "Except I imagine you're feeling bad enough to put you off doing that again. What on earth—?"

"Gillie," James's dad interrupted. She looked up at her husband, and James saw them exchange a warm glance.

"Okay, I've finished." She gave James a mischievous look. "Glass of wine, James?"

James groaned, and the others laughed.

"Unkind, Gillie," Laurie said, though James could see a smile on the corners of his lips.

"And how much did you have, mister?" she demanded.

Laurie's laughing admission that he had, perhaps, been less than sober himself helped bridge the gap; and Laurie and Al's conversation about films took over most of the lunch. They argued a little, as they always did; but James knew from the sparkle in both sets of eyes that they enjoyed the tussle. And James was able to sit back, drink water, and force down as much food as his queasy stomach would allow, in peace. Thanks to Al's actions, in fact, the awkwardness between James and Laurie was kept to a minimum. James apologised to Laurie later for getting so drunk, and Laurie assured him that nothing too embarrassing had befallen him.

"I suppose...you won't want to do it again, sometime? If I promise to drink a bit less?" James said ruefully. He knew he was indeed the idiot Al said, but no matter what the situation, he still wanted to spend time with Laurie. Even if next time, he'd make sure to sit on the other side of the table. Safer that way.

Laurie smiled. "As long as your mother doesn't think I'm too much of a bad influence."

"I'll come too," Al said brightly, "to keep you both in check."

Laurie scoffed and told him to wait to be invited, but nonetheless, James knew that it was a sincerely meant statement. Al had clearly resigned himself to the inevitable, which James was grateful for; he'd worried that Al would say out loud that he didn't think Laurie and James should see anything further of each other, and that would have been hard to explain. When he muttered something appreciative to Al later that evening, Al shrugged it off.

"Clearly, it's pointless expecting you to be normal over Laurie," he said. "I've given up trying. Still think you're an idiot, mind."

"Yeah, so do I." James sighed. "And thanks for helping. I think Laurie's fairly convinced. Though I'm pretty freaked out; since when were you the one getting me out of scrapes?"

Al gave him a crooked smile. "Yeah. I think I owe you a few," he acknowledged.

"And I've got the message." James tried not to sound as unhappy as he felt. "Laurie isn't interested. Not even vaguely. I swear I've finished trying."

"Laurie," said Al, giving James a brief snog, "is even more of an idiot than you are. If possible. But yeah, sadly, it seems that particular message needed to be got."

In fact, James reckoned his parents got more in the way of explicit affection from Laurie than James himself did. His mother certainly did, but Laurie was close to James's dad, too, and they'd started spending hours in the garden together, sorting out the vegetable patch. Terry was finding it difficult to manage alone this summer; James suspected that there would have been precious few vegetables if it weren't for Laurie's help. James himself had always hated gardening; he wondered whether he was a disappointment to his father in that way, but Al had made a rude noise when he'd broached the subject.

"Don't be ridiculous. Your dad thinks you're the best thing since sliced bread. Probably better than sliced bread, actually. Now, if you'd only take your guitar out and play to him when he was tending to the carrots, or whatever the fuck he does out there, he'd probably be in heaven."

James had scoffed, but he had noticed that his father really did seem to appreciate his music, and he was spending longer downstairs, playing in the same room as his parents than he'd done since he was fourteen years old and desperate for encouragement. And it seemed Al was right—Terry had turned to him one night and said, "I'm glad you've started playing to us again. I've missed it."

James's father was an unemotional type, unlike Gillie. A man of few words, unlike Al. To have him mention something so specific was oddly touching.

"Thanks," James had said, giving his father a rare hug.

If only Laurie felt the same way. James had taken his guitar out to the garden on a few occasions, as per Al's suggestion, but he felt self-conscious quite quickly. Not always, but not infrequently, Laurie would make excuses after James had been playing for a while and go inside. He'd reappear again later, but he was always very quiet. After a while, James took the hint and only played outside in Laurie's absence.

Chapter Seven

IN MANY WAYS, James was sorry to return to university. He loved his course and he was fond of his friends in Surrey, but the summer had been good and James was beginning to suspect that he was rather a homebody on the quiet. Plus, he'd always missed Al when they'd been apart, and after a summer of, quite frankly, pretty brilliant sex, he had another reason to miss his best friend. Which was something that he certainly wasn't going to be explaining to any of his housemates—the Rainbow House crew had agreed to live together in third year too, to the pleasure of them all.

But James was sorrier still that he'd gone back to uni when he came home at Christmas. His father's health had been getting worse, he knew, hence the fact that he had taken early retirement that summer. But it was a shock to see quite how ill Dad was looking. James was used to the stairlift, but he wasn't used to his dad needing a wheelchair both at the top and bottom of the stairs; his father was now completely unable to walk unaided, and James had to turn his head away to hide his tears when he saw his mum cutting up Dad's Christmas dinner for him.

"There are new lesions," his mother quietly told him later. "Large ones."

"I see."

There were too many words James couldn't say. *He's dying, isn't he?* How could he say that to his mother, whose love for Dad had always been so clear, so strong—so happy? Terry's MS had never been the relapsing-remitting variety most commonly known and with the best known outcomes. But there was a world of difference between knowing your father had a life-threatening illness and actually seeing it threaten his life. James was glad to have Al there, though they said little about it.

James had wondered, after a term away, whether the 'thing'—whatever it was—between himself and Al would have fizzled out. They'd looked at each other for a moment when he'd first arrived home—Al was already round at his house, looking as if it was more his own than James's—and there had been a moment's silence before Al had grinned broadly and pulled him into his arms.

"Hey, Jamie, so good to see you," he'd said.

"Ditto." James had plenty of friends at uni, but none like Al. Mind you, there was *no one* quite like Al.

"I'm on your floor, since Laurie's here over Christmas," Al informed him.

James took a deep breath. "Convenient," he said, cocking an eyebrow at Al.

Al's quirk of the lips told him all he needed to know. "Dating your right hand all term, Jamie?"

James raised two fingers at him but didn't deny it. It was the truth, after all. And James hadn't been wrong about sex with Al. It was as satisfying as ever, and Al more than willing to oblige. James wasn't quite sure what Al got out of the deal, but when he mentioned this to his best friend after receiving a particularly enjoyable blow job from him, Al just grinned.

"You're not that awful in bed, Jamie. At some point, you might notice I'm enjoying myself. And, thank fuck, you have no expectations that I'm suddenly going to want to take you on dates. Trust me—it works very well for me. What's more, if and when you find yourself a decent bloke, Laurie or not, I will fade cheerfully from the sexual scene." He considered a moment. "Well," he corrected, "from *your* sexual scene. Not the one in general."

James couldn't repress a snort of laughter at the idea of his taking Al on a date, and the conversation dissolved rapidly from there. The sex, however, continued.

When it came to Laurie, however, far from staying 'over Christmas', James noticed that the other man appeared practically to be living with his parents. Perhaps it *was* just his usual Christmas stay, but James wasn't so sure. When the new year came and went and Laurie showed no sign of leaving, James was certain there was more to it. Broaching the subject with his mother, he got confirmation.

"Yes, darling," she said. "He's been helping. With Dad."

"That should be my job," James said, a horrible feeling twisting in his gut.

His mother smiled sadly. "No. It shouldn't. It shouldn't be Laurie's, either, but somehow... Well, anyway. He insisted, and apparently your father and I weren't strong enough to say no."

James swallowed. Aside from the devastation over his father, there was something else stirring. The same feeling he'd had all those years before, watching Laurie rescue the bird from the netting. The realisation that Laurie really was the amazing, wonderful man James thought him. A squirmy sensation in his stomach moved lower still, pooling in his groin.

"I...I'm glad. That you've got him," he forced himself to say. Then, "Mum, I can stay. I don't have to go back to uni this term."

Her hand cupped his cheek, and though there was sorrow in her eyes, her smile was as warm as ever. "Yes you do, darling. If for no other reason than because your dad is so proud of you. Never forget that, dearest. Dad thinks—he knows, just as I do— that you are fantastic."

James had bent his head down onto his mother's shoulder, and if he had cried a bit, she was careful never to show that she knew.

Chapter Eight

THE CALL HE'D known was coming arrived in mid-February. The weather was cold, and James's mood colder still. He looked down and saw his mother's number on his mobile.

"James." Gillie's voice was broken with despair, and James knew at once what the call was about.

"Mum, no."

"He's not dead yet, darling, but...it won't be long. Come home." James could hear his mum trying not to cry, for his sake. That hurt nearly as much—no, it didn't; but it was hard, nonetheless, even though he loved her for the effort. "Laurie's driving down. He'll pick you up in an hour or so. It'll be quicker."

"How..." James choked, and coughed, and tried again. "How long has Dad got?"

His mum's tone was soft. "No more than twenty-four hours. You'll be glad of that when you see him. James dear, I'm so sorry."

"Mum..." There was so much to say and yet nothing to be said at the same time. "I wish I was there with you. With Dad. I shouldn't have come back to uni this term."

"Yes, you should," his mother said quickly. "Dad would have hated you to stay home. You know that. He's so proud of you, dearest."

The words brought tears to James's eyes. He blinked them away and said nothing.

"Laurie will be there as soon as he can. He's already left. He'll text when he's close. And James..."

"Yes?"

"I love you," Gillie said.

"Love you too, Mum," James said, but she had cut the connection.

James was glad that he and Laurie had become comfortable in each other's company again that summer. Although he had no energy to waste on awkwardness or embarrassment, it would have added a layer of stress, which he could do without. The drive was a silent one nonetheless; James could think of nothing but his father, and Laurie let him be. When they reached the hospital to which Terry had been admitted, James barely managed more than a brief thank you before heading straight for his mother. Al was sitting by her side, looking oddly gentle and quiet. He was the first to see James, and he touched Gillie's hand, directing her attention to her son. Gillie was in James's arms within seconds, one hand stroking his head as she had used to do when he was a child and had fallen and hurt himself. These days, however, she had to reach up rather than down to do it. Since when had his mother become so small?

"Dad?" he asked.

She nodded. She looked exhausted, worn down with sadness. "Through here."

When he saw his father, he understood what Mum had meant. Terry was gaunt and grey, and looked more dead than alive already. It was also clear, from the drips and medication charts, that he was in considerable pain, though he didn't show it. Only just conscious, he yet had a smile for James.

"James. Things must be bad," he whispered. "Collared doves at my vegetables again?"

"Worse," James said, blinking back tears as he hugged his dad. "Wood pigeons."

"I know why people eat pigeon now," Terry said, trying to smile. "It's nothing to do with taste, just to keep them off the veggies."

"Love you, Dad," James said.

Terry managed the smile he'd been trying for, but his eyes were flickering shut even as he did so. James was half-glad; it meant that the tears he'd tried to suppress could fall down his cheeks as he looked at his father.

"Love you, Dad," he whispered again, knowing—perhaps knowing, even then—that it might be the last chance to say it.

His father died two hours later, his wife and son by his side, his adopted son and wife's best friend outside the room.

Al never spoke of what he and Laurie had done in that time; James never really cared enough to press him. But there was, in some way, a greater understanding between the two after that. Later, Al would say, "Yeah, maybe he's not so bad," and James would know it for the high praise it was. But just at that moment, it didn't matter.

A week later, James returned to university for the last three weeks of term. He did it at his mother's request, and he knew he wasn't making the best use of his time when he was there. Nonetheless, he knew also that she had a point. What use was sitting at home moping going to be? Gillie herself had to return to work, and in some ways James suspected it was the best thing for her. Dad was gone. Dad was gone—no, Dad was *dead*—and he wasn't coming back. Not now, not ever. All his life, James had known that this was a possibility, but somehow he had never really believed it. Even at Christmas, he had sort of...hoped. A faint, pathetic hope, but the hope of someone who had needed to believe in magic.

Magic had failed him. His father was dead.

His father was dead.

James had never realised, not really, what a close relationship he had with his parents until half of it was gone. He remembered the summer, remembered Mum and Dad's response to his getting allegedly so drunk he had no idea how he got home. The look on his uni friends' faces when he'd mentioned that his parents had known about such an occasion had been a sight to remember. "You didn't tell them…" (Peter.) "Your mate told them? Didn't you kill him?" (A squeak of horror from Jenny.) "No way would I tell mine." (Peter, again.)

Worse, though, was their response to his father's death. He'd come back to university after the new year, knowing it was likely, and the bracing comments, now that Terry had died, of "It's the best thing" and "Well, you knew it was coming" made him want to turn round and murder someone, even though he knew his friends were trying their best to be comforting. Hell, perhaps it was a great thing for his studies—god knew he didn't want to go out with people who thought that the 'best thing' that could have happened to his dad was that he'd died. James had spent the three weeks before the Easter break working until his brain was fuzzy, until he could sleep without wanting to cry about his daddy—because how fucking juvenile would his college friends think him if they knew about that?

The coming of the Easter holiday was a relief. Al had texted, telling him that he was intending to be staying over at that time, too. It was expected, now, but James had still been glad to hear it. Still been glad to know that some things were the same, even when everything was different. It *was* a relief, but it was still hard, going home. Knowing that Dad wouldn't be there. His mother met him from the station and pulled him into the tightest hug he could ever remember from her. He held her close in return, noticing how much weight she had lost in just a few weeks. She felt fragile in a way she never had before, and James didn't think it was merely physical.

"It's so lovely to see you, James," she said, as if she hadn't seen him for months—years—rather than weeks.

"You too."

So much unsaid, but they climbed quietly into the car and headed back to the house. Al and Laurie were both there. James raised his eyebrows a bit when he saw how settled Laurie looked.

"Yeah," Al agreed, below his breath as he gave James a hug and then pretended to put him into a headlock, "I'm on your floor again."

"Hmph."

James found himself watching the way his mother and Laurie interacted. The way, that evening, Laurie quietly massaged her shoulders as the four of them sat in front of the television watching *University Challenge* and shouting out the answers that they knew. It had been a family tradition for years. James discovered that his time at university had taken away a little of his skill at the game as he was out of practice, and it was curious to have Laurie rather than Dad answering; the sorts of questions he knew the answer to were of a very different type, though James felt his heart squeeze in his chest when some gardening questions came up which Laurie answered correctly. That would be a result of last summer, Laurie and Terry working together.

Occasionally, Laurie disappeared for a while. James, drifting into the kitchen with a vague intention of washing up, caught sight of him outside the back door and pushed it open. Laurie was leaning against the wall, a packet of cigarettes in his hand, extracting one.

"You don't smoke," James said. It was perhaps not the most tactful introduction, but he'd been taken by surprise. He'd known Laurie—well, most of his life, pretty much—and he was pretty sure the other man had never smoked.

"Apparently I do now," Laurie drawled. He stuck the packet back in his pocket and pulled out a lighter.

"Oh." James thought about this. Knew it was his father's death—hell, possibly the months beforehand, when Laurie had been living with James's parents, doing the things that James should have been doing—which must have persuaded Laurie into this habit. He felt unutterably guilty. "I wish you didn't," he said unhappily.

"Sorry, James," Laurie said, half-mocking. "I didn't realise I needed your permission."

James flushed. "I don't... I mean, I didn't..."

"Don't worry about it," Laurie advised.

He flicked the lighter and lit the cigarette. Leaning back, he put it between his lips and sucked hard, a tiny moan of enjoyment leaving his throat as he breathed out the smoke. James had a sudden, vivid flash of what it might be like to have Laurie's lips around his cock, Laurie making that noise as he sucked hard on something very different to a cigarette. His body reacted predictably, and James, mortified, turned away.

Laurie chuckled softly. "That bad, eh? You can't even bear to watch? Your mother brought you up well."

James didn't turn round. His errant cock was still hard, and his mind just *would not shut off* the visions of Laurie. He knew his face was burning red, too, but that was the least of his worries right now. Think of something else. Think of something other than Laurie's mouth, the way he'd moaned...the way he'd *moaned*. Oh fuck.

"It's not like that," he said, his throat constricted. "I was just going to go back inside and wash up, that's all."

He pushed back through the back door with more haste than politeness, trying not to visualise himself leaning back up against the wall as Laurie had been doing, Laurie on his knees in front of him, his mouth...

The washing up would have to wait. James had a sudden change of plan, going quickly upstairs and running a shower. Which of course he was using to cool off, not as a place to wank in privacy. Laurie's hands had always done it for him before—those large gentle hands. James had always been able to imagine Laurie putting them all over him, touching him and making his skin tingle with sensation. Now his mouth too? It was too much. It was too bloody much. James came hard, leaning against the shower wall and hating himself for being so lacking in self-control when it came to Laurie. Living in the same house as him was torture.

"Unexpected shower," Al murmured to him on his return downstairs.

James gave him a look. "Don't," he said through gritted teeth. "Just don't."

Al's face lit up in amusement, but he was sensitive enough to say no more, though his gaze flickered between Laurie and James a few times that evening, his mouth curved in a small smile. Well, at least James was providing someone with some entertainment. Bloody Al. Bloody Laurie. Just at that moment, James hated pretty much everyone.

Over the days that followed, a pattern emerged. Laurie was at work during the day, as was Gillie, quite often. But in the evenings, James would watch Laurie with his arm around Gillie's shoulder, chatting in an undertone to her; making her cups of coffee; hugging her affectionately when she went to bed. Every so often disappearing—and now, James knew where and why. And his mind—not to mention his cock—went into hyperdrive every time Laurie left the bloody room. It was fucking humiliating; that's what it was.

But he had other issues, too. Sometimes he woke to hear voices in the room which had once been his parents', and knew that Laurie was in there with his mother. James would look over at Al, sleeping soundly, and sigh. On the one time he'd kicked Al awake to talk it through with him, however, Al had been unimpressed.

"Yeah, she probably can't sleep." He rolled over and glared blearily at James. "She probably didn't kick him awake, though."

"But it's 2:00 a.m."

"Yes, precisely—and some of us were asleep," Al grumbled. He dragged James back down from a sitting position. "Stop worrying about Gillie and Laurie, and go to bloody sleep."

But it nagged at James in the deepest corners of his mind. Sure, Laurie was his mum's best friend, but this was...wasn't this overkill, somehow? He was *in her bedroom.* And...and, he was everywhere, and he was touching her all the time. Finally, when he and his mother were alone in the kitchen, the words just started spilling out.

"So, Laurie," he said, leaning his arms on the counter and looking at Gillie with a frown.

Her eyes softened and she smiled. "Yes. He's a tower of strength, that guy. I don't know what I'd do without him."

"Ugh, Mum, stop it. Just stop it."

Gillie looked up, surprised. "Stop what?"

"He's always here, all the time. What, have you moved on from Dad so quickly? Onto the next bloke?" James demanded angrily.

His mother turned a face of such utter disbelief on him that he was shocked. "He's my best friend, James. In case you hadn't noticed, I lost my husband just over a month ago, and I need someone. I don't know what went on with you and Laurie, and I thought you'd sorted it out. Apparently not. I didn't ask because you asked me not to, but"—her voice was getting louder and louder as she continued to speak—"for once in your life, can you stop being so fucking selfish?"

James took a step backwards. It must have looked ridiculous, a six-foot young man cowering away from his much smaller mother, but it wasn't a moment to consider something like that. If Gillie had hit him, he couldn't have felt worse. His mum was by no means a perfect mother, and she'd yelled at him before, but nothing like this. The worst thing was knowing that he deserved it. No, he corrected himself—the worst thing was watching his mother's face crumple as she clung to the side in the kitchen as if she needed to hold on in order to stay standing and burst into tears.

James realised there were tears on his own cheeks. He took a couple of clumsy steps towards his mother, putting his arms around her and mumbling "I'm sorry, I'm sorry" over and over again into her hair.

Gillie hugged him back, sobbing, for a few minutes. Then, with characteristic determination, she began to recover herself. "No, love, I'm sorry," she said quietly. "I didn't mean to shout. I know you've just lost your dad."

"I shouldn't have said what I did," he muttered, leaning his head on top of hers.

"No," Gillie agreed. She pushed him away a little bit so that she could look up at him properly. "Your dad and I got together when we were eighteen years old and just started university, love," she said gently. "I loved him so much. I never stopped." James felt an awful sense of familiarity about her words. Would it be the same for him and Laurie? Still, Dad had at least loved Mum back. James had nothing. But he was silent and let his mother continue. "We knew this would come," she said. "That's why we married early, had you. People thought we were mad, marrying at twenty-two. But your father had already been diagnosed by then, and they warned him it would kill him in the end. We didn't know how long we'd have." She sniffed and wiped her eyes, turning to switch the kettle on. "Cup of coffee," she said. "We had twenty-five years together, all in all. Good times." She smiled at her son. "You. But if I need a best friend to hold my hand, to help me through, don't read more into it than that, James. I don't even know how to go on living without your dad."

She turned to the side, bustling around to find cups and coffee powder. James knew she was crying again and was wracked with guilt. It had been such a stupid thing to say, but he'd just been so jealous. Coming home, always seeing Gillie in Laurie's arms. Where James wanted to be more than anything. How could she not want him? James always had.

"Mum, I'm sorry," he said again, awkwardly.

"I know." She reached up, patted his head. "I love you, darling."

"Love you too."

Chapter Nine

"YOU SAID WHAT?" Al demanded later, as they were sitting in James's room that evening. "Bloody hell, Jamie, I hope she tore you a new one."

"Thanks. I can always rely on you to make me feel better," James said. He was sitting on the floor at Al's feet, leaning his head against his friend's knee. "I know, I know, it was fucking stupid."

"Offensive," Al corrected him. "Are you an idiot? Wait—don't answer that. You just asked your mother if she was sleeping with a much younger guy a month after your dad's death—oh, and the bloke in question happens to be gay, to boot. You're officially an idiot."

"She must've thought about it, though," James said defensively. "I mean, Laurie's..."

"Don't," said Al quickly. "Please don't go there. I really don't want to think about your mum in that way, not with Laurie."

"You'd do him, wouldn't you?" James accused.

Al ran a hand through his messy hair. "Wouldn't say no," he admitted. "At least, I would—because you'd bloody kill me, but if circumstances were different..."

"I'm an idiot to ever have thought he might be interested in me," James said.

"Hey," Al pointed out, "I'd do *you*, too. In fact, I am. Anyway, you're much more of an idiot for still being hung up on him despite the fact that he's not interested. And more still for asking your mum... I still can't believe you did that."

"Nor can I." James sighed. "I apologised. Profusely."

"I should think so too," Al said, as sternly as Al got.

"Yeah, well. I'm going to bed."

"I'd better come too, save waking you up later." Al stretched and ambled off to the bathroom without saying anything further.

Although officially Al was sleeping on a mattress on the floor in James's room, in practice they both always ended up in James's bed. James half wondered what would happen if his mum looked in one morning and saw them there, but it had been years since she'd been in his room without waiting for him to invite her in, so the chances were low. Anyway, she'd probably just presume that it was a comfort thing, nothing more. And she might be right, at that. James and Al were having sex, sometimes, but it wasn't regular. James just appreciated having someone there with him—it felt so weird being at home and Dad not being there, and knowing that Dad was never going to be there again. God knew what it must be like for his mother. James felt guilty all over again.

Al returned, and James got through the bathroom, coming back and stripping everything off before pulling a T-shirt on. Al himself had a particular collection of ratty old T-shirts he wore in bed, usually ones to do with Star Wars, or Avengers, or one of his geeky interests. Today's just had 'Male—Female—Geek' with a symbol for each one. James shoved him over in the bed and got in beside him.

"Which are you today—male, female, or geek?" he asked.

"All three, if I want to be," Al retorted. "Gender binary's a load of bollocks, anyway. That's why I only wear this one in bed these days."

"You'd know." Al identified fairly contentedly as male, but James knew he'd had plenty of experiences, sexual and otherwise, with people whose gender didn't necessarily match what had been written on their birth certificate. "Though surely that's gender trinary—with geek as a separate gender altogether?"

Al raised his eyebrows and nodded. "Possibly. That could work. Not all the nonbinary people I've slept with were geeks, though—it is possible for me not to sleep with fellow geeks, you know."

"Me?" James suggested.

Al snorted. "You! You're just as bad. Just because you keep your Harry Potter obsession under wraps these days doesn't mean I don't know it's there. I saw you reading fanfiction the other day."

James blushed. It had been *explicit* fanfiction, at that.

"Anyway, you were doomed from birth, what with Gillie and her sci-fi and fantasy stuff everywhere."

"I should've rebelled by being terribly normal," James said regretfully. "I missed an opportunity there."

Al glanced at him. "I think you've done enough rebelling for one day, don't you?"

James groaned, putting a hand to his head. "Did you have to remind me? Fuck. Don't know how I'm going to face Mum in the morning, let alone Laurie. I escaped up here the moment he arrived. Embarrassed."

"He doesn't know."

"No, but I do. God, I hope Mum doesn't tell him."

"She won't," Al said confidently. "You know she won't."

"Yeah." James turned away, suddenly feeling lost and alone again. "I don't want this, Al," he said quietly. "I want my dad back. I want this all not to be happening."

"I know, Jamie," Al whispered, holding him, kissing his hair. "It's okay."

"It's not."

"No," Al admitted. "It's not. It sucks. It's bloody awful."

He kissed James gently on the mouth, and James responded, needing something. Needing the distraction of sex, of forgetting about everything but his body and Al's and the way they felt together. James stroked a hand down Al's back, and Al made a little noise of agreement and pulled him closer, so that their bodies were touching all the way down. Then it was all James, all James's grabbing hands, demanding mouth. Touching, holding, insisting. Frotting against Al until they were both hard and gasping, and then reaching for condom and lube, ripping into the package viciously and shoving it over his hard prick. Then he was slathering his cock with lube, pushing inside Al without anything in the way of preparation for his partner. Al gasped but didn't complain, arching his body back and letting his muscles go slack. And James fucked him hard, over and over, biting more than kissing him, demanding everything Al could give him and then taking more. Hard and fast and angry and sad—all the emotions that were racking James's mind, coming out through his body. Cathartic sex, with Al still muttering his name, as he always did when they fucked. Sometimes James wondered whether Al ever got it wrong—called out the wrong name when he was having sex—but he never did so with James. James came in a burst of stars and fury and helplessness, his body shuddering and shaking and then—finally—relaxing. He pulled out and removed the condom, but didn't even bother cleaning himself before he fell asleep, still lying across Al, his weight probably crushing the smaller man. At last, he'd found a temporary release from his troubles.

James woke in the morning to find Al out for the count next to him. Clearly at some point in the night, he'd rolled off his friend; he had one arm still flung over him, but that was all. Al looked younger when he was asleep—he'd always looked a little young for his age, but he'd made up in spades for that with his attitude. No one who'd met him for more than ten minutes ever patronised Al. James wondered what went on in Al's mind to make him the way he was. What he got out of sleeping with every Tom, Dick, and Sally he met. James then thought about his own situation. Ironic, really, that he'd wrongly accused his mother of sleeping with her best friend—when that was precisely what James was actually doing. But that was different, he reminded himself. Totally different. He hadn't just lost his partner of twenty-five years.

Twenty-five years. Laurie would be in his midfifties in twenty-five years' time. Would James still be mooning about after him then, or was he at some point going to get a grip and let go of this ridiculous obsession? Would Al still be sleeping with every other person he met? Would James's mum have found someone else, settled down with them? She'd not quite be seventy—she'd got a lot of life still left to live without his dad. But it was too early to think about things like that. James slid out of bed carefully, making sure not to wake Al, and went to the bathroom to clean off the remains of the night before. He'd been bloody selfish last night, he told himself severely, realising that he didn't even know if Al had come or not. James had been too wrapped up in himself. Al hadn't complained; James knew that he wouldn't complain, either, but it was still unacceptable. Not saying no didn't necessarily signify consent, after all. Still, it was probably par for the course for yesterday, he thought, all things considered, turning the shower on so that it was hot enough that it stung his skin.

Dressed and downstairs, the first person he bumped into was Laurie, who was sitting at the kitchen table nursing a cup of coffee.

"Oh. Hi," said James, brought up short and never at his best before he'd had a large coffee in the morning.

"Hey. How are you doing?"

Laurie looked tired and a little rumpled, but strangely, it suited him. He looked approachable. Touchable. James wished he hadn't thought that. He looked away quickly.

"Fine," he said briefly, boiling the kettle. It boiled fast; Laurie couldn't have made his long ago.

"Sure?" Laurie was giving him a long look over the top of his coffee, an expression of concern on his face. He hesitated and then went on. "Gillie said you were—"

"Was what?" James asked, immediately defensive.

Laurie shrugged uncomfortably. "Struggling a bit. Understandable."

"Oh, what, my dad's just died and I'm not on my best form? Apologies for that."

"Yes, I know. It's hard on you."

"Harder on Mum."

"Equally hard," Laurie said quietly. "She's a brave woman. Still, it can't be great timing for you with finals coming up. I guess at least you've got your friends around you."

James gave a bitter laugh. "Yeah. It's all fun and games in Surrey, you know. Fucking fantastic. I'm having a whale of time there. Because it's great having everyone talking and then shutting up the moment you come in just to make absolutely sure you know they've been talking about you. And then to turn to you and all they want to do is talk about it, and all I want to do is not. And," he added viciously, "if anyone else tells me that 'Well, he was ill' like that makes it okay, I'm going to punch them in the head. Like if you're ill, you might as well be dead anyway."

"James." Laurie reached out and put his hand on top of James's. It was warm and large—larger than James's own, though James had long slender fingers. "Don't."

"Don't what?"

Laurie curled his fingers into James's palm. James wanted to hate everything right now, but he couldn't hate the way that it felt. Instead, he hated the fact that he didn't hate it.

"Nothing. Grieve in your own way," Laurie said, keeping that warm, strong grasp of James's hand. "I just—if you want to talk, I'm here for you, too, not just Gillie. I know you've got Al, but if you want me..."

James tried not to think about the possibilities in those last four words. He looked at Laurie unhappily. "Why?"

Laurie gave a huff of surprise. "Because—because—" Unexpectedly, he looked away for a second, as if the question was awkward to answer. "Friends do that?" he suggested.

"And we're friends?" James asked cynically, thinking of everything that had happened, wondering if his mum had told Laurie what he'd said about them.

"I hope so," Laurie said. "I hope so very much."

And there was something in the tender, caring way he said the words that made James suddenly, unexpectedly, start sobbing. He hadn't expected to do any such thing—hadn't cried much at all really since the beginning, the guilty tears yesterday aside. But this—big, heartbreaking, gut-wrenching sobs... They seemed to come from nowhere. And once they had started, it was very hard to stop. Laurie put his other arm around James's shoulders, still holding onto his hand. He didn't say any of the usual platitudes— it'll get better with time; everything happens for a reason; what doesn't kill you makes you stronger.

Instead, he just held him, and when James's sobs had begun to calm a little, he said simply, "I'm here with you."

"I'm sorry," said James, eventually.

"Nothing to be sorry about," Laurie said matter-of-factly.

"Yeah, there is. I've been a bastard to Mum lately. I don't know why you're even talking to me at all."

"You're saying that. She's not said it. She's just mentioned you're finding it tough—which is hardly surprising," Laurie added.

"It's so shit. Dad—just—argh. And my friends at uni think I ought to be getting over it by now." James hadn't even told Al that, scared, maybe, that Al might have agreed privately, even if he would never have said it out loud. "Especially 'because he was sick'."

Laurie's arm tightened for a second around James. "Any of them been through it themselves?"

James shook his head.

"Then they're talking rubbish. Do you remember what a fuck-up I was when my mother died eight years ago?"

James frowned. "I remember it happening. Not you being a fuck-up."

"Yeah, you do," Laurie said. "I was over here so much, crying on Gillie's shoulder, that you and Al asked me if I didn't have a home to go to."

James grunted. "Oh, great, I have a track record of being a bastard to people who are grieving."

Laurie laughed at this. "Oh, I think you were being sympathetic in your own way. At least, that's how I tried to see it at the time. When I could see at all through the tears. I was a right mess."

"Were you close?" James asked. "I don't really know anything about your family."

There was a pause. Then Laurie swallowed hard. "No," he said at last. "We weren't close." He was silent again for a second, before continuing. "She didn't approve of me studying Film Studies. It wasn't serious enough for her. She wanted me to do accounting, or medicine. Law. Something important, worthwhile. When she died, I was working for the council in a job I needed the bare minimum of qualifications for. It proved her point in her mind. She didn't like the fact I was gay, either. The way she saw it, that meant no career, no babies. No future, basically."

Fuck. James had never known any of that. "God," he said awkwardly. "I'm sorry." The question would out, though. "Why'd you care so much when she died, then?"

"You know I've got no dad. She was my family. All of it." Laurie let go of James as he spoke, like he'd suddenly realised he still had his arm around him. He picked up his coffee again and drained what was left of it. "And she died thinking I was a failure." He gave James a small smile. "That hurt, James. Even now, when I've got this lectureship, I find myself wondering whether it'd be enough. Whether she would think that was good enough for 'a son of hers'. If she knew me now, whether she wouldn't be ashamed of me." He got up, carrying his cup to the sink where he made a big deal of washing it out. "Anyway. Forget that. It's water under the bridge. A long time ago. But don't think I don't know how hard it is when a parent dies, okay? And I owe Gillie, big time. She probably kept me from ending up hospitalised with depression—and no, I'm not joking about that."

James felt like the biggest git alive. Laurie had lived with all that, and he'd never known. Never thought to ask, really, about Laurie's family. At least James's dad had loved him. Loved him to bits, in fact. James hadn't even had a moment's doubt about that. Hadn't even considered it, in fact—which was really fucking privileged of him, especially considering Al's dubious parenting.

He swallowed and made the effort. "I know she's really grateful that you're here now. And"—it was hard to say, but he realised it was true—"and I'm glad she has you." He changed the subject, feeling awkward. "How do I make it up to Mum?" he asked abruptly.

Laurie didn't say anything about the sudden switch. "You don't need to."

"No," agreed James, "I don't need to. But I want to." Laurie had turned from the sink and was now facing him again. "Something I can do for Mum and you. Thanks for this morning, by the way."

"What, for boring you with my family history?"

"You didn't bore me," James was saying as Al walked into the kitchen.

Al looked between the two of them and raised his eyebrows. "Sorry. Interrupting something?"

"No," said Laurie casually. "James was just thinking of something nice to do for Gillie."

Al's bright eyes flicked between Laurie and James again, a different expression in them this time. James gave him a glare, and Al looked innocently back at him.

"Sounds like a great plan," he said in response. "What'd you think of?"

"Hadn't got that far," James said.

"He's only just sprung it on me," Laurie added.

"Hm." Al frowned. "Why don't you make her something? A cake or whatnot."

The other two looked at him with varying expressions. James looked thoughtful, Laurie disconcerted.

"You know, that's not a bad plan," Laurie said, unflattering surprise in his voice.

Al grinned at him. "I'm not just a pretty face. People like things that have taken an effort," he added to James. "You at least owe her the effort."

James gave him another warning—and slightly beseeching—glare and got a reassuring nod from Al. "Yeah," he admitted.

"It's not just because you like cake, is it?" Laurie asked.

"Your lack of faith pains me," Al said, giving Laurie a hurt look. "Jamie can make almond cake if he wants"—almonds being one of the few things Al didn't like. "I'd even offer to help, except—" He looked at James, and the pair grinned.

"What?"

James gave a muffled snort. "Have you ever seen Al's cooking?"

"Ah." Laurie smiled. "I see. And I apologise for the baseless accusation, Al, too."

Al shook his head sadly. "You know, it's important to trust other people's motives. Sometimes, people just mean well." He kept his eyes fixed on Laurie, but James knew the comment was meant for him as well, and he flushed.

"Yeah, shut up," he said, giving Al a shove. "You can talk to me whilst I bake. But we'll have to wait till Mum's gone to work."

"Yes. And I am sorry, Al." Laurie came over on his way out of the kitchen and ruffled Al's hair. "I'm beginning to realise there's more to you than meets the eye."

Al gave a wicked grin. "Oh, you'd better believe it," he said. He ran a shameless hand down Laurie's arse in suggestive fashion before letting him go, earning himself yet a third dirty look from James.

Al laughed.

Chapter Ten

THE LAST TERM passed as last terms do. Exams, and stress, and—well, more phone calls with his mother than perhaps most final year students had, but James didn't give a fuck any more what the rest of them thought of him. He had friends enough, even if they smiled patiently at him in a way which made it clear that they were putting up with his vagaries rather than understanding where he was coming from. He had friends, and he had loved his years at university. He'd heard from others that their best friends came from those days, but truthfully? He couldn't imagine anyone but Al as his best friend, no matter how many others he made. Mind you, Al had always been more like a brother—well, perhaps not in certain ways, James thought, thinking of the many times they'd fucked—than *just* a friend.

He tried not to think of Laurie at all—a pathetic attempt, which failed on a near-daily basis, but that was another matter— but he knew that his disinclination to form any sort of romantic relationship had been another thing which had made him stand out as odd in his friendship group. Still, at least he—unlike Jenny, poor girl, who was devastated after Eloise had dumped her three weeks before finals started—had no new romantic worries to cope with, he reminded himself. And if the loss of his father was not something which he could just 'get over', no matter how much his friends hoped for it, he could at least hold it down. It was a pain inside now; something which was there—a bit like his love for Laurie—but which he felt he had some control over at most points. Love and death. The unmentionables, he thought ruefully. And at least his mother had accepted his apology (and cake) and whispered that she understood, she understood; that he should not worry about Laurie and her. James hoped very firmly that his mother did *not* understand— but at least he knew that she had forgiven his burst of ridiculous jealousy.

Two months later, he was home from university for good and all. Results would not be out for another six weeks, but with exams done, it had been time to come home.

The first thing he noticed was Laurie's absence. Gillie's quiet "Yes, he left a few days ago" brought guilt bubbling to the surface. James knew damn well why Laurie had left, and it was due to him.

"Mum, he didn't have to—"

His mother hugged him close. "Love, he has a home of his own," she teased, making light of it. "He knows he doesn't need to be here if I've got my boy back. Not that you're a boy," she added, smiling. "My incredibly grown-up son. And no, that doesn't mean you can't move out next week if you want to, by the way. But oh, James, it is so good to have you back close."

"It's so good to be here," James said—and meant it.

He had applied during the last few weeks for a place on a music teaching diploma course and was waiting to hear back about that. It was a two-evenings-a-week thing, so he would be able to have a job meantime, travelling into London for the teaching, taking the exam at the end of the year. The composing? God knew. He'd keep writing things—couldn't help it. The music just happened, whether he wanted it to or not. Maybe nothing would ever come of it, but he'd be stunted, somehow, if he didn't compose. If he didn't sit there with his guitar, playing tunes no one had ever played before—knowing that he'd created something new.

"And Al?" he asked.

Gillie's face closed like a shut book, which was disconcerting. It was not, after all, a usual expression when she was speaking about Al. What on earth had his friend done, James wondered in alarm?

"He'll be here soon, I think. Tomorrow."

"What's he done?"

His mum forced a smile. "Al's done nothing. Sorry, love, I didn't mean to worry you."

"What's wrong, then?"

"Let him tell you," she said.

So James did.

Al had his final exam the next day, his room in the shared house paid for until the end of the month. *Much as I love you, Jamie,* the text had said, *can I wait till tomorrow to see you?* James had understood at once, and it had been...not nice, because Dad's absence was a blight over everything he and his mum did together...but good, somehow, just to be him and Mum that one night. She'd said she'd cook, but James had insisted on helping, and somehow they'd ended up with something nearer a banquet than a sensible dinner.

Al's appearance the next afternoon was the next big thing. Final exam over, Al was bouncing with even more than his usual amount of manic energy, almost bubbling over with words and ideas and enthusiasm.

"Hey, Jamie," he yelped, pulling his best friend into a big hug and doing a sort of dance simultaneously, nearly bringing them both crashing to the ground. "We're out in the world of grown-ups now."

"My considered opinion," Gillie, who was sitting watching the boys, said, "is that anyone who still calls them 'grown-ups' isn't one."

"You do," James accused, looking round at his mother.

"Precisely," she beamed. "Hello, Al."

"Hi, Gillie." Gillie got an equally enthusiastic hug from Al, though fortunately without the risk of toppling over, since she had the sense to stay sitting. "Thanks for having me back again."

She frowned at him. "I do wish you'd stop saying that," she scolded. "James doesn't. I don't see why my other son feels the need to."

Al nudged her in a catlike fashion with the side of his head. "I don't deserve you," he said, in an unusual fit of humility.

"No," she corrected, "what you don't deserve is—" but she cut herself off. "Anyway, lovelies, how about some sparkling wine? Yes, I know it's only half past three, but you're both home and you've finished your finals, and it's about time we had something to celebrate, isn't it? Why don't you two go and sort yourselves out—Al, you'll need to put your things away—and then we will reconvene down here in an hour or so and get merrily pissed. How does that sound?"

"Gillie, you are an angel in human form," Al said happily.

"And whilst you're getting sorted, you and James can talk about all the things we mere mothers don't need to know," she teased.

The young men exchanged glances as they made their way upstairs with Al's bags. "Sometimes your mum is a bit too close to the truth," Al said, a rueful grin upon his face. It seemed that everything would come with some sort of smile attached today.

"She's pretty good," he acknowledged. "So, how are you doing? I won't ask how your exams went. You've probably aced them all because you're obnoxious like that. And anyway, they're done and gone now. What I really want to know is what Mum thinks you don't deserve, and why she clammed up every time your name came up before you got here."

They pushed their way into Al's bedroom.

"Oh." Al pulled a face, kicking the door shut behind them. "It's nothing important." He stopped short at that and sighed. "Okay, it is. Since it's you. Gillie asked if I'd be here over the summer, and I said that I wasn't sure because I was going to see if the parents wanted me over there for a bit. Haven't seen them since the end of my first year, after all. But yeah. Turns out the answer is no, the last thing they want is to see me."

"Bollocks," said James, sitting down heavily on the bed and finding himself somewhat at a loss about what to say in response to that. "That's...that's shit. What did they say?"

"It wasn't good timing, blah blah blah, house in uproar, very busy...no, Christmas wouldn't be any better," Al said briefly. "Guess it's good in a way. It tells me all I need to know, and I can stop bothering to try."

"Bloody hell, Al." James leaned over and gave Al a tug, pulling him half into his lap. "That's bloody awful," he said. His arms closed around his friend.

He kissed the top of Al's head, and Al lifted his face to kiss him back rather more demandingly, before pulling away and saying, "I'll get over it. It's just... I knew they weren't keen on me, you know? But it was pretty much 'We don't ever want to see you, thanks'. I even offered to pay for flights."

"Yeah, cos they're short of a bob or two," James grumbled. Al's parents, if not stinking rich, were certainly beginning to smell a little.

Al shrugged. "They've always been funny about money. Thought it was the least I could do. And at least I know now it's not that. It's me."

"They're absolute tossers," James said bluntly. "I'm sure I'm not supposed to say that about someone else's parents, but they shouldn't act like absolute tossers if they don't want me to say they're absolute tossers. Can I get 'absolute tossers' into this comment any more times, d'you reckon?"

"Not without sounding like an absolute tosser," Al said, with a small smile. He reached up and kissed James again. "Thanks, Jamie. And your mum's been fab. She didn't quite say 'absolute tossers', but she might as well have."

"Oh, Al." James pulled Al closer still, other feelings swelling inside him—other parts of him swelling outside him. "God, we want you." He nuzzled the side of Al's neck. "In more ways than one."

"Please, Jamie," Al said simply, turning his mouth and pressing it demandingly against James's.

They were just supposed to be having a chat, getting Al settled in. If James's mother came up now, god alone knew what she'd think. But James found that he really couldn't care about that right at this moment, not with Al pressed against him, not with the mix of anger against Al's parents, affection for his best friend, and a rising sexual need growing inside him. James responded fiercely, trying to put all the things he couldn't say into the kiss. Al groaned and turned on James's lap, pushing him back onto the bed and lying sprawled across him. One hand was in James's hair, tugging his head firmly up against Al's own; the other stroked down his side and tucked under his hip, anchoring them together.

"Al..."

"Fuck me. Please?"

James had never heard Al sound so pleading. He knew logically that Al must enjoy having sex with him—they'd done it enough times, after all—but James had always felt, really, that it was for his benefit, not Al's. Al had so many other lovers; he'd also made it clear enough that if James ever found a real partner, whether Laurie or someone else, he'd fade into obscurity without a moment's concern, would be delighted for James, in fact. But right now, Al was clinging to him and begging James to fuck him, and the vulnerability he was showing hit James hard. James was one of the few people whom Al ever allowed to see him vulnerable, and even so, it was rare.

"Yes. I've got you."

He pulled away from Al just far enough to strip Al's top off, followed by his own. Then he slid down, kissing and nibbling Al's chest; running his tongue across one of Al's nipples over and over until Al bucked involuntarily beneath him.

"God, yes, that. James," Al whimpered.

Al's hands were greedily exploring James's back, tugging hard at his hair. He had twisted his legs around James's, and as James continued his ministrations against Al's chest, Al began to jerk his hips rhythmically against James.

"More. Please," he whispered.

James's hands fell to Al's jeans. He undid them, before tugging them off ruthlessly, along with his pants and socks, so that Al lay naked on the bed. Sitting up, he went to unbutton his own, but Al pushed his hands out of the way and replaced them with his own smaller ones, then made short and efficient work of unfastening James's trousers. Instead of pushing them off, however, Al just slid his hand inside James's pants. He grasped his cock, and stroked it with firm, determined purpose.

"Fuck, Al." Al was too good at that. James's eyes flickered closed for a second, and he had to fight to keep them open and concentrate on what he was doing—what he wanted to be doing. "Where d'you keep the lube and condoms?"

It was weird to be fucking in Al's bed; it had always been James's. James wasn't sure, now, why that was; frankly, he didn't care much right at this moment.

James shoved his trousers down as Al replied, "Top drawer." Then, with a smile, "Same as you."

James laughed and retrieved them. He pushed his clothes to the floor, and lay back on Al, whose hand was still touching his cock with those practised movements, which were sending James to the edge.

"God, that... I need to fuck you," he murmured, leaning down. He took Al's mouth in a bruising kiss.

"Yes." Al looked up at him with intense green eyes. "Do me hard, Jamie."

James looked back at him for a second, wondering what was in Al's mind. It was difficult to concentrate with Al stroking him like that.

"Turn over," he said.

Usually they fucked face-to-face; sometimes James on top, sometimes Al taking control. This time, James knew, Al needed James to be in charge; to feel that this was something James was doing because he wanted to. Al needed to feel wanted, to feel needed. And fuck, was he both of those things. Al made a little noise of assent and let go of James, turning onto his front.

"On all fours," James instructed.

"God, Jamie."

Al obeyed, and James, after covering and slicking up his cock, pressed gently on Al's back so that he was on elbows and knees, his legs spread apart.

"Want you so much," James said quietly, running his hands down Al's surprisingly muscular back.

"Fuck, just—" Al whined with frustration.

"I am," James reassured him.

He ran slippery fingers around Al's entrance, sliding just the tip of one in. And Al cracked.

"I just—please, Jamie," he pleaded. "Please, god, just do me. I need you inside me. I need to feel... Just, oh god, James, please."

James swallowed past an unexpected lump in his throat and switched fingers for cock, pushing deliberately into Al. Al's body gave a little resistance but then welcomed him in as if it had been made solely to take James's cock.

"Fuck, that's—"

"Fuck me," Al urged again, rocking against James with increasing desperation.

On another occasion, James might have teased him a little for this; this time, however, he pressed a kiss to Al's back and then began to move. Al gave a sigh of relief and gratitude, rutting back against James and giving as good as he got. James reached round and began to jerk Al's cock, and Al started to make those little noises that James had begun to know so well, followed by a litany of semi-coherent words and phrases.

"Yes, James, Jamie, fuck. God, I...please...oh yes, yes, like that...hard, harder, oh...*oh*..."

James knew he wouldn't last long, not at this rate; not with Al this needy and wanton, pushing and begging. He'd never fucked Al quite this hard before, with no care for how Al might feel afterwards. It was so clear that this was what his friend wanted, however, and fuck, it felt good. Thumping into him so hard, his hand gripping Al's hip tightly enough that it would probably leave bruises. Al begging, *begging* him to do it more. James's thrusts became more uneven as he got closer, his concentration waning. He pulled harder on Al's cock, determined to make him come before James reached his own completion. Al cried out louder and came in a warm rush over the bed and James's hand, half sobbing. James pushed a few more times, watching the sweat spread on Al's back, the way he threw his head back as he orgasmed, how in those few seconds he was nothing but what

James made him. It was enough. James groaned into his own orgasm, coming hard, buried as deeply in Al as physically possible. His arms held Al tightly to him, and they stayed like that for—James did not even know how long, before Al sighed and slid down onto his front, James perforce following. The air was full of the smell of sex and the sound of heavy breathing as the two young men fought to catch their breath. James could have lain there for some time, breathing Al in, holding him close, but he knew his weight would be heavy on Al. He knew, too, his friend and lover's likes and dislikes. Therefore, James rolled Al onto his back and gave him a quick hug before sitting up.

"We want you, Allie," he said.

Experience had taught him that Al was uncomfortable with too much in the way of post-sex cuddles. The affectionate diminutive of his friend's name was about as far as he dared go. He used it rarely—Al would, James reckoned, probably commit murder if called 'Allie' often; but he would also recognise the sentiment behind its occasional use.

Al, his breathing still a little ragged but his temperament restored to normal, snorted. "You just want me for my body," he retorted with a small grin.

He wiped his face; James wondered whether it was just sweat or whether there really were tears there as well. He wouldn't ask, and Al wouldn't tell.

"Nah," James corrected him, grinning also, and following his friend's lead to a lighter mood. "That's just an added bonus." He hesitated. "You're okay? Seriously?"

Al dragged his T-shirt back on and rolled onto his side, then propped one elbow on the bed and leaned his head on his hand. "Yeah. Don't worry, Jamie. I'm not going to do anything stupid." He gave him a quick glance, the sombre mood not entirely gone, it seemed. "No need to hide the knives or anything."

The comment wasn't quite as sarcastic as it sounded. No one but James and Al knew about the time when they'd been sixteen or so. James had wandered into Al's room to find his best friend sitting on the bed, a wicked-looking serrated blade in his left hand, his right wrist exposed, looking from one to the other with an obvious intent and purpose.

"Al, what the hell…"

Al hadn't looked up. He'd said, his voice toneless, "I could just do it, Jamie. It wouldn't take much. Make everyone's lives a lot bloody simpler."

James had lunged across the bed at that, tearing the knife from Al's hand.

"No. No, it wouldn't. Al, stop it."

"I honestly can't see why not." Al had looked at James, not tearful, not even looking that upset. Looking, in fact—to James's severe discomfort—almost peaceful. "So much easier, Jamie."

James had stayed awake all night with Al, almost forcibly inserting him into pyjamas around midnight, before settling down for the long haul with his friend. Al hadn't said a lot, but it had been more than clear that he had been—quite literally— deadly serious. He'd ended up staying at James's house for the next fortnight after James had cornered his mother and informed her privately that he was pretty certain that Al would not stay at his own parents' home if he left theirs. If Gillie had presumed that James meant that Al would run away, it was still enough to persuade her to let Al's visit continue. And although James had never seen Al with a knife again—not in *that* way, anyway—neither young man was likely to forget the episode in a hurry.

"Good," James said now. "Now, weren't we supposed to be sorting ourselves out and going and drinking sparkling wine with Mum? Rather than having sex and then deep and meaningful conversations? Not that I'm complaining about the sex, mind you—"

"You didn't seem to be," Al interjected, amused.

"But—well, wine."

Al stood and stretched. "Yeah, sounds good. Shower first?"

"Is that an invitation?" James asked with a grin.

"Good god, Jamie, you are in a good mood." Al laughed down at him. "If you want. If you think you could handle it."

"*I* could...not sure Mum could if she came up. Might be a bit hard to explain," James said thoughtfully. "Okay. After you."

Chapter Eleven

THE NEXT EXCITEMENT, such as it was, was the exam results. James had known he was pretty sure of a second-class degree—the question had only been whether it would be an upper or lower second. Discovering it was the higher classification was pleasing, especially in the circumstances of his somewhat disturbed final year. James's tutor had told him that he could put in an Extenuating Circumstances form if he wished, but James had chosen not to do so. Although his father's death had made a massive difference to his life, he wasn't at all sure that it hadn't made him more determined to do well rather than less. Happy with his upper second, then, James was amused and delighted, but not surprised, when Al emerged with a first-class degree.

"Swot," he teased, and Al laughed.

"That's what they get when they ask me to do things I'd've wanted to do anyway. In any case, yours is from a proper university."

"That's nonsense," James said dismissively. There was still a tendency in some places to rate certain types of university above another, but it was not something James had any time for. "I'm pleased with my result, especially given the shit that went on this year—but you? You got a bloody first, mate. I hope you're pleased."

Al had a certain tic when he was shy or embarrassed, ducking his head a little. If you listened to what he said, he always claimed to lap up praise, but when it actually came to it, he was made a little uncomfortable by it, however pleased he was.

"Yeah," he admitted a little sheepishly. "Not bad."

"So, Al," Laurie greeted him when they next met, "PhD on the agenda?"

Laurie had been avoiding the house for the week before the results were published, uncomfortable with the fact that he'd known Al's grade before Al did. But he was back now, looking genuinely thrilled by Al's success.

"Oh hell, no!" Al said hastily. "I'm not academic. Anyway, didn't James tell you? I've got a job. Fen's taken me on permanently at the wine shop."

"Of course," said Laurie, "a degree in Film Studies is important training for selling wine. Surely you're going to do something with your degree? You know most of the others on your course would kill for a first?"

"Yes, Daddy," Al said meekly. "I've got ideas; don't you worry."

He wouldn't say more, not to Laurie, but he'd shared some of his plans with James. The job at the shop was, in fact, part-time—a deliberate move on Al's behalf. He was working enough hours to cover his living costs, so long as he was frugal, but he had given himself enough time for other projects. He had continued to love film-making, and a lot of his first-class degree was due, James suspected, to his solo project in his final year, in which he had created a short film from beginning to end. He was currently looking at the possibilities for getting it shown on a small scale and was working on the script of a new film, which he hoped to get financial support to produce. Looking at his friend's combination of skill and determination, James was pretty sure that Al would be successful. He was, nonetheless, bashful about it—especially when it came to Laurie. Al had always claimed not to give a toss what Laurie thought of him, and for a long time, bound up in his own feelings about Laurie, James had believed him. Now, however, he wasn't so sure. However, Al had earned the right to his privacy, so James wasn't going to be giving him away.

It was a peaceful summer, all in all. James did the rounds of all of the music tuition shops in the area, explaining about the course he would be starting in September and making contacts. A couple of places said that they would keep him on their books and contact him if anything came up; they seemed impressed by his dedication to completing a course in teaching to go with his music degree. Several asked him to play, and one offered him a job working in their shop on the basis of his guitar talent, something he took up willingly. Laurie teased him gently about the fact that both he and Al had completed good degrees in order to work in shops, but James, remembering the conversation they'd had after his father's death, politely reminded him of council jobs requiring five GCSEs, and Laurie laughed and laid off.

Al moved out in August to the smallest bedsit James had ever seen. James was intending to live at home for the foreseeable future; he got on well with his mother, and he knew she liked his company. After his father's death, he couldn't quite bear the thought of leaving her to live all alone—not yet. Though 'alone' would perhaps have been a misnomer. Gillie had introduced another inhabitant to the house in the shape of Roger, a fluffy ginger kitten—something which had almost been enough to persuade Al, who was particularly fond of cats, to stay put. James and Gillie teased him that he came round to visit Roger rather than them, and Al grinned and didn't deny it. James could have done without the trail of destruction that the small animal left in its wake, but looking at his mother's face as she watched Roger cavort around the sitting room, he could not complain. And Roger formed an immediate and extremely strong bond with Gillie, greeting her on her return from work with a purr much too loud for an animal of his size and rubbing round her legs until she petted him. James would have put up with an awful lot to see his mother smile like that. And yes, all right, the kitten was rather sweet in his own way.

James did take a week off work near the end of September, just before his new course was due to start, to visit his friend Jenny from university. She, too, had moved back home—Peter and Donna were still living in Guildford, but like James—albeit for different reasons—Jenny had a strong affinity with her home. Hers was much more place-related, whereas James's was people-related. Jenny had an abiding love for the area around Carmarthen in Wales, the town on the outskirts of which she had grown up. It had been good to see Jenny again and really interesting to meet her parents and see the area where she'd spent her childhood. Very different from James's London upbringing. She'd confessed that she'd found Guildford a bit of a shock when she first came to uni. James, having seen the rugged mountains and beautiful countryside of her home, could not be surprised. Nonetheless, glorious as it had been, he had to admit that he preferred living a bit closer to the centre of things. He'd have hated to live in central London, but the outskirts were perfect—big enough to have a decent garden—but near enough that it was only a five-minute walk to the nearest tube station. He could be in the middle of London whenever he wanted to be.

And it was where his mum and Al and—yes, all right, even now, even after all this time—where Laurie was. Perhaps that last ought to have been enough to encourage James elsewhere so that he could get over this bloody ridiculous obsession, but he'd been away for three years at university, and it had failed dismally to make even the smallest dent in his feelings for the other man. At least here, he could have some sort of friendship with Laurie. And if that was all he could ever have? Very well, that was all he could ever have.

It was 3:00 p.m., and the late September sun was shining down as James arrived back from Wales. It was nice to be home again. James's mum had texted him, telling him she'd arranged a barbecue—*I know it's a bit late in the year, but we didn't have one all summer, and it seemed a waste to let the whole of the good weather pass*—so he wasn't surprised when he saw Al in the garden. He made a detour on his path to the front door to say hello to his best friend, who was sitting lazily back in a chair, a beer in his hand.

"You're here already, then?"

"Nope, I'm just a figment of your imagination," Al retorted. "I ought to warn you that I'm also staying over, so you're not getting rid of me in a hurry, either. I know your family's barbecues—they go on forever, and I couldn't be arsed getting home again."

"Sounds wise." James frowned. "Don't know what it'll be like this year, though."

Without his father. He didn't need to add that bit. Al knew it all too well.

"Some things won't change," Al assured him, his expression sympathetic but his words brisk. "Laurie's here, by the way, and he's staying too, so I've stuck my bag in your room."

"Where is he? Come to that, where's Mum?"

"Where d'you think? Laurie's talking to Gillie about something. You know what they're like when they get started with one of their heart-to-hearts. I decided to stay out here with a beer. Seemed safer."

"Good idea," James agreed. "Fair enough. I won't disturb them if they're in the middle of something, just dump my stuff. Back in a minute."

He went into the house and immediately heard his mother's voice emanating from the sitting room. "Oh Laurie, I wish you'd talked to me about it," she was saying, her tone full of the loving sympathy it always held when Laurie was in trouble.

James nodded to himself. Al had been right—this was one conversation not to interrupt. He'd got as far as the fifth step before he was caught short by Laurie's response.

"What was I supposed to say, Gillie?" Laurie demanded. "I'm not exactly likely to ask 'What do you think I should do about the fact that I keep fantasising about fucking your son?'"

James turned abruptly. He dropped his bag as he jumped back down the stairs, then stormed into the sitting room in one fluid movement. "*What?*"

Laurie looked at him with total horror, face flushing scarlet. "Shit," he said fervently, turning away so that his back was to James.

James's mother looked between the two of them, her face carefully neutral as she said, "Hello, James. Welcome back. I hope Wales was lovely—you can tell me about it later. Well, I think I'll leave you two to sort this out between you."

She left the room, but James barely noticed. His attention was all on Laurie.

"What did you just say?" he demanded furiously.

Laurie wouldn't turn round. James could see that he had both hands pressed hard to his face. "Do we really have to discuss this?" he muttered. "You were not supposed to hear that."

"You didn't precisely keep your voice down," James pointed out. "So would you like to tell me what the fuck you meant by it?"

The answer was clearly no, as both of them knew. They also knew that James wasn't going to let that be an option.

"I think it's fairly self-evident, isn't it?" Laurie took a deep breath and turned to face James, dropping his hands to his sides. "There wasn't much room for mixed messages."

"Past or present?" James asked.

"Do we have to?" Laurie said again, looking wildly round for a way to escape.

"Past or present?"

"Both," Laurie mumbled. "Happy now?"

"Bloody ecstatic," James said sarcastically. "Did it ever occur to you to mention it?"

"It's been occurring to me *not* to mention it for quite some time," Laurie shot back.

"How long?"

"Why do you think I broke up with Kieran?" Laurie said. He was tapping his fingers on his thigh in an impatient tattoo.

"What the fuck? That was years ago."

"Well spotted."

"But when I—" James broke off. "It was after that when I pretty much threw myself at your feet, and you told me to fuck off, for god's sake."

"*Yes.*" Laurie glared at him. "You were this kid I'd known since you were ten, and I was fantasising about fucking you, and it was so bloody wrong. I had a boyfriend; we were living together, and yet I was thinking about this *child* I'd known forever, and who was the son of my best friends. I felt like an absolute creep, all right? A dirty old man who should know better. And then you kissed me, and I freaked out, like I must have infected you with—" He stopped, wiping his face with his hand, wiping tears away. Tears, for James.

James felt his own eyes prickle in response, and he fought it back firmly. Instead, he said, "I was nineteen, Laurie. The same age you were when you got to know Mum."

"That was different. That was friends. Plus, she hadn't known me as a kid."

"And again? When I was nearly twenty-one?"

Laurie looked hard at him. "I thought you didn't remember anything about that," he said.

James had the grace to look a bit embarrassed. "Yeah, well. The point is, you moved away so quickly, you could've been in a different country within five minutes. It wasn't something I exactly wanted to remember. And you were hardly acting like you had any interest in me."

"You were in a bloody relationship!" Laurie retorted. "And drunk as all hell. You'd hardly have kissed me otherwise." He swallowed, looked away again. "Look, I don't have to stay for the barbecue. Gillie will understand. In the circumstances."

"What?" James was honestly bewildered.

"We can't sit down like nothing has happened now and pretend everything's okay, can we?" said Laurie. His head had dropped, and he had stopped tapping his fingers.

"I thought..." James moved a pace closer to Laurie. "I thought you said—present?"

"Yeah, well, that makes it all the more awkward, doesn't it?" said Laurie grimly. "I'm not going to sit there eating steak and burgers, with you wondering whether I'm thinking about your cock."

"Would you be?" James asked, finding a smile begin to materialise on his face.

"James, for fuck's sake!" Laurie said, his voice breaking.

James was silent, and Laurie looked up, finally. James moved a pace closer again, so that he was right in front of Laurie. Slowly, giving Laurie all the time in the world to move away, he put his hands on Laurie's shoulders. Laurie was an inch or two taller than James, which was something James wasn't used to. When you were six feet tall, most people were your height or smaller. But with Laurie, James had to lift his head a little. Instead of kissing him, however, he stood there and waited.

"James?" said Laurie, his tone tentative.

"Yes? I'm not drunk now, you know. And single. Very, very single."

James was so close that he could feel Laurie's breath against his mouth. He parted his lips a little and looked at Laurie. And waited some more.

Please. Please.

Laurie kissed him. It was the most uncertain, wavering kiss James had ever received. As if Laurie was waiting every second for James to push him away. As if James hadn't been spending the last six years hoping for this to happen. James kissed back, and he felt the moment some of the tension left Laurie—the moment Laurie's arms slid around him, grasped him in the small of his back, and pulled him close.

And then...? It went on forever. Or for a second. Both, at once. James could have drowned in Laurie's kiss, have stayed there with their mouths together for the rest of his life. And it was over, suddenly—a moment after it started—a lifetime after it started.

"Still?" Laurie asked, his voice breathless.

James wrapped his arms around Laurie's neck, laid his head on his shoulder. "Still. Always."

Laurie bent his head down and rested it on James's shoulder in turn. "I thought...you'd find someone better. Someone younger. More interesting. More...not me."

James breathed deeply. "You're that stupid."

Laurie's hand came up to caress James's cheek. "You could do better."

"What if I don't want to?"

"Ah." And James could feel Laurie's smile against his face. "Well, if you don't want to..."

The hand on James's cheek became more insistent, pressing his head towards Laurie's. Pressing his mouth against Laurie's. Laurie kissed him again, more certainly now—more demandingly.

"Laurie," James murmured as they broke apart.

"If you don't want to find someone better," Laurie whispered against his skin. He pulled James close. "God, James, if you still want me..."

"Please," James said softly. "Please."

Laurie gathered him in, and James had never been with a man who could do that—who could surround him, crush him close against his body like this.

"Tell me to stop. Tell me to stop, James, or I swear I won't," Laurie said, his words interspersed with kisses on James's neck, on his hair, on any part of James he could reach.

"Don't. Don't ever stop." James tugged Laurie closer—as close as they possibly could be, with their clothes on, in the middle of James's mother's sitting room. "I want you so much." He hesitated, the thing he couldn't—shouldn't—say still there, hovering on the edge of his tongue. "I love you so much," he said, throwing the last of his pride—the only part left from three years ago—down in front of Laurie, waiting for it to be trampled into the ground again.

Laurie had never said he loved him. Only that he thought about sex with him, about fucking. James loved Laurie with every fibre of his being, in the way which was only meant for love songs and the sort of stupid bloody books and films that he hated. True love conquers all? True love was a myth made up to make people hurt like James had been hurting for the past years. What was Laurie supposed to do about that? Wanting to take someone to bed—as Al proved so regularly, so very regularly—had nothing to do with love, with romance, with forever and hearts and all the senseless, ridiculous stuff in James's head.

Laurie buried his head deep in James's hair. So deep.

"I love you," he said. "James, if you...if you change your mind—you're so much younger—I'll understand. I don't expect...forever. But I can't...I can't stay away any longer. I can't pretend that...I don't...love you. If it's just...if it's just today...tomorrow... I don't care. I..."

"Oh, shut up," said the man who had loved Laurie for almost six years without reciprocation, without hope, without anything.

Laurie held him so close it was as if he was trying to burrow into him, as if he was trying to make them one person, not two. And James clung back with all his might, part of his brain still insisting that no, this couldn't be happening; no, this wasn't real.

It was real. It was Laurie.

"Come to bed," James said pleadingly.

Laurie took a half-hearted look out of the window. "They'll be expecting..."

"Come to bed."

"Yes."

James threaded his fingers through Laurie's and pulled him towards the stairs, where he almost fell over the bag that he'd dropped there when he'd heard Laurie's words. Half an hour in which the world had totally changed. He picked it up, and Laurie followed him to the bedroom, where James shut the door on the outside world with a thump. It was just James and Laurie now, no one and nothing else. Laurie's hands went to the bottom of James's T-shirt, a questioning look in his eyes, and James nodded and raised his arms to allow Laurie to take it off. Laurie followed suit with his own and then pulled James back against him. They were skin to skin for the first time, Laurie's arms holding him, and James shook with the intensity of the sensation.

"James?"

"Sorry." He pressed his head against the side of Laurie's. "Wanted this for so long. God."

Laurie's grip tightened. "Here now."

He manoeuvred James over to the bed and lay down on it with him, still keeping him tightly bound up in his arms. His mouth moved to James's, and they kissed again. Laurie's legs tangled around his own; Laurie's hands glided over his back as if he needed to touch every single piece of James.

"You're so bloody gorgeous," Laurie whispered in his ear between kisses. "So gorgeous."

James had run out of words. All he could do was feel, taste, touch. Laurie moved down his body, kissing his neck, his chest. He grazed his teeth against James's nipple, and James heard himself moan, as if it were coming from another person. Then Laurie's tongue was exploring the planes of James's stomach, his fingers fiddling with the zipper on James's jeans. He ran a row of kisses along the point where the jeans met flesh before pulling down the material. Always so slow, always giving James time to say no, if James had been able to say anything. As if James would ever have said no to Laurie, ever.

"Oh god," Laurie said when James lay exposed in front of him. There was an expression on his face that James had seen nowhere before—almost of awe. "Please, James."

"Anything," James said hoarsely, so totally out of his depth.

Laurie lowered his mouth to James's cock with a little sound of need. Warm mouth. Laurie's warm mouth. James groaned and bucked up involuntarily, and Laurie swallowed him down further, sucking and licking and running his tongue across James until James could do nothing but moan and fight for breath. His whole existence had faded to this—Laurie's lips around his cock, one of Laurie's hands stroking his balls whilst the other ran up his chest. And Laurie continued to do marvellous things with his mouth, and James was orgasming hard, harder than he'd ever done, his head spinning, his brain shorting out because it was too much, too much.

When he had recovered himself enough to see again, Laurie had slid back up next to him and was kissing his neck over and over.

Laurie, James realised, was still in his trousers; this seemed overdressed, and James stumbled through trying to find the words to tell him so, finally settling on, "Trousers? Off?"

Laurie kissed him before complying, and James could taste himself on Laurie's mouth—the taste of sex and come. But then Laurie had shrugged his way out of his trousers and pants, and James's attention was distracted because Laurie...Laurie's cock was enormous. James swallowed, suddenly considering the feasibility of having it inside him, when he'd had no one inside him before. He'd been waiting—foolishly, he'd thought, all these years—for Laurie. Waiting for this. What if he disappointed him?

"Okay?" Laurie asked. There was a little tremble in his voice, as if he was still uncertain of James.

James nodded. "Yes." He looked at Laurie's cock. "Shall I...?"

He went to move down the bed to take Laurie in his mouth as Laurie had taken him. But Laurie put a hand on his shoulder, holding him back.

"Touch me," he said, that tremble still there. "Please? God, all those times I've watched you playing your guitar, thinking about what it would feel like to have you looking at me with that expression, your hand on my cock, your fingers..."

James reached out and wrapped his long fingers around Laurie's cock. It was heavy and hot and glorious. "I thought you didn't much like my guitar," he said. "Sometimes when I was playing, you used to walk aw—" He cut off suddenly, as a new interpretation of this occurred to him.

The new possibility was confirmed by the look on Laurie's face. He was blushing dark pink. "Yes. Well. Do you know how humiliating it is to have to lock yourself in your friends' bathroom whilst you wank over their son, just because you've watched him strumming a guitar?" He lowered his head, apparently unable to meet James's eyes.

James's hand stroked up and down Laurie's cock. He revelled in the size, the feel, using his other hand to stroke the base, running light fingertips against Laurie's skin until he heard Laurie's breath falter.

"You wanked over me?"

"Too much," Laurie mumbled.

"Like this?" James continued to pleasure him, spreading the precome over Laurie's length, his hands faster and slower, harder and gentler, trying out the different feelings and watching what it did to Laurie. His own cock began to harden again, just a bit.

Laurie looked back up at James, his lips parted, his breathing ragged, his eyes full of love. "Nothing like this. This is...god...amazing. Please, James."

"I thought—hoped—you were going to fuck me," James said, his heart beating faster.

"Only if you—don't mind."

"Mind? God, Laurie." James gave a little breathless laugh. "Only been waiting six years."

He leaned over to his bedside cabinet and dug out lube, still keeping one hand firmly anchored to Laurie's cock. He felt like he couldn't bear to let go, even for a second.

"Six?"

James looked at him, shamefaced. "Ever since you first brought Kieran home. I was so bloody jealous."

"I didn't know."

"Good."

Laurie looked back at the bedside drawer. "Protection?"

"I've always used it before, but...do I need it?" James couldn't help the stupid, sentimental part of himself which wanted—just this once, this perfect first time—to forgo the usual paraphernalia.

"No, but..."

"I trust you," James said simply. Because it was that simple.

He slathered some lube on his hand and then passed the tube to Laurie, wrapping his slippery hand back around Laurie's erection. "Um, go slowly, though, yeah?"

"Been a while?" Laurie asked quietly.

James looked away, unable to look Laurie in the eyes as he spoke the words he never thought he'd say aloud. "I... I've not... I've never..."

He risked a glance back at Laurie at this admission. Laurie was looking down at him with something bordering on awe.

"You've never done this?"

"I've had sex," James said defensively. "I've just..." He bit his lip, hard, the mild pain somehow reassuring that he was here, that this was truly happening. "I was...waiting..."

"James." Laurie spoke very softly. "Look at me." James could feel his face flushing as he looked at Laurie. "We don't have to do this," Laurie said, touching gentle fingers to James's face. "There are plenty of other things—"

"I want to," James said quickly. He swallowed. "I mean, I've wanted to—for years. There's a reason I've not done it before." He looked Laurie steadily in the eyes and saw the moment that Laurie understood what he was saying; that it was he whom James had been waiting for.

"And you'll trust—" Laurie broke off, breathing fast. Then, his voice suddenly husky, he said, "Pull your legs back for me, James. Let me touch you."

James let go of Laurie reluctantly, spreading his legs wide. Laurie squeezed the tube over his fingers and slid his hand between James's parted thighs. There was something in the way Laurie looked at him which made this almost unbearably intimate—something more than just preparation for sex. Laurie pressed a finger against James's entrance, running it round the edge and across the small sensitive ridge at the base before pressing it inside. James's cock stirred a little more, and Laurie smiled at him and stroked it gently.

"Feels good," James said, taking a shaky breath.

Laurie played with the finger, sliding it back and forth, in and out, until James was writhing.

"More?"

He nodded, and Laurie slid another in beside it, curving them round until they pressed against the sensitive spot inside James. He made a noise something like a whimper, his cock springing thoroughly to life as Laurie stroked inside him.

Then Laurie was moving again, scissoring the fingers to open James up, and James was crying, "Oh please, oh please..."

"May I?"

Laurie positioned his cock and slid his fingers out, his gaze still checking with James that it was okay. James hitched his hips, pushing himself against Laurie, offering himself up. Laurie pushed in carefully, little by little. James groaned. God, Laurie was big. It hurt a bit, but at the same time, he wanted more. Fuck, this was actually happening.

"Too much?" Laurie asked anxiously.

"No. Perfect. Please."

James was rubbing his own cock with the hand he'd used to lube Laurie's. The slip-slide of that and the sensation of his muscles relaxing into Laurie's penetration were making any pain disappear beneath a glorious pleasure. Laurie pushed in further.

"God, Jamie, you're so tight," he said, sounding like James was the most wonderful being ever. "So good. Oh god, so good." He had his arms on either side of James, and James could see the muscles trembling with the effort Laurie was putting into staying still. Laurie's breathing was jumping about, stuttering and starting. "I need to move," Laurie said desperately. "Please, James."

"Do it."

James could watch Laurie's face all day like this, lit with desire and tension and need; falling apart because of how much he wanted to be inside James. Falling apart for James. Laurie thrust all the way in, and James flinched a little, but his muscles were already adapting; and Laurie was pulling out a little bit and then moving back in, and somehow—

"Put your legs round me," Laurie said urgently, and James wrapped his legs around Laurie's shoulders. "Yes, like that," Laurie breathed, and this time when he moved, he hit that place, the one which made James see stars, the one which made him want to scream out Laurie's name and beg him to do it again and again.

But Laurie already *was* doing it again, and James, almost without realising it, was crying his name out—"Laurie, Laurie"— and touching Laurie's face, as if making sure he was really there. Laurie was silent; there was just the harsh heavy sounds of his breathing, and the noises his body made as it pressed against James, as he fucked into James over and over, with James's every repetition of his name. The stars were taking over all of James's vision, and he could feel every inch—every single last inch of Laurie inside him—and he had waited so long for this, so long.

And Laurie cried out "James" just once, and James could feel his lover pulsing inside him, coming for him. Coming *in* him. His hand worked his cock faster, and then James was coming too, for the second time, spilling across his belly.

Laurie collapsed beside him, his cock slipping out, and he pulled James almost fiercely to him, holding him so close. They were hot and sticky with sweat and come, and James had never felt anything better than this in his life. Than holding Laurie, all messed from sex and murmuring incomprehensible half sentences about 'James' and 'Wonderful' and 'Can't believe'…

How long they lay there, James wasn't sure, but eventually—regretfully—he stirred.

"Suppose we ought to go outside, really," he said reluctantly.

"Mm." Laurie pulled back a bit to look at him. "You do know that your mother will know exactly what we've been doing, don't you?"

"Maybe she'll just think we've been talking," James said optimistically, though he had a feeling that Al would have his own suspicions, now that Laurie mentioned it. He'd be fielding the results of *that* one later, for sure.

But in some ways, Laurie knew James's mother better than James did. "She'll know," he assured him.

"Oh." James blushed. "Right."

"Just thought you ought to be warned," Laurie said. "You don't regret it, though?"

James looked at him as if he were mad. "You're kidding! Do I look like I regret it?"

Laurie smiled slowly, and James smiled back. He knew his expression must be unbearably smug right now, but he couldn't help it.

"No," Laurie said. "You don't. Quick shower?"

"You going to come with me?" James asked daringly.

"If you'll have me."

They kissed in the shower, still unable to stop touching each other, still unable to believe that they could do this. They kissed getting dressed. They kissed on the stairs. They reached the door to the garden, and Laurie hesitated. James kissed him again for good measure, and Laurie smiled.

"Okay. Okay. We can do this."

"We can." James put an emphasis on the *we*. He slid his hand into Laurie's, threading their fingers together. "Come on."

Hand in hand, they walked across the garden. Gillie had joined Al, who was leaning back with his feet on a second chair, laughing at something Gillie had just said. Al glanced up and saw Laurie and James, and a look of delighted amusement crossed his face. James glared at him, daring him to say anything. Gillie looked up at them both.

"Oh, splendid. Al was just getting hungry," she said brightly, avoiding any attempt at broaching the issue of what had been going on.

"Al's always hungry," Laurie said, doing his best to follow her lead, as he so often did.

Gillie laughed. "True. Can you give me a hand with the barbecue, Laurie, please?"

"Mmhmm."

Laurie gently disentangled his hand from James's and went over to join her over the grill. James's gaze lingered on him, still scarcely able to believe that this was his boyfriend. He heard a meaningful cough from behind him and turned to look at Al.

"So?" Al raised his eyebrows, and James went over and perched on the edge of the table—slightly cautiously—his arse was undeniably sore.

"What?" But his blush had given him away.

Al cackled. "Ha! I knew it. How was it?"

The answer to anyone else would have been 'None of your business.' James had a feeling that the answer to Al should have been the same, but a lifetime of sharing pretty much everything with Al made that impossible.

"Good. Better than good. Amazing."

"As good as me?" Characteristic Al.

James grinned. "Yes."

"Good." There was a slightly disconcerting genuineness in Al's response in the circumstances. James's best friend grinned back at him. "Pity if you'd pined over him for six years and he was a disappointment."

James looked over to where Laurie had just placed the third steak on the barbecue. He felt his heart do a funny sort of flip, the type that they said in books that it could do but he'd never quite believed was real. Laurie. Oh god, amazing, impossible, *his* Laurie.

"Not a disappointment, Al," he said softly, finding it hard to believe how much he loved Laurie still, after all these years, how incredible it was that they could possibly be together. "Not a disappointment at all."

About the Author

P.A. Friday fails dismally to write one sort of thing and, when not writing erotica and erotic romance of all sexualities, may be found writing articles on the Regency period, pagan poetry, or science fiction. She loves wine and red peppers, and loathes coffee and mushrooms.

Email: penfriday@gmail.com

Website: http://www.penelopefriday.com

Twitter: @penelopefriday

Facebook: http://www.facebook.com/penelopefriday

Also by P.A. Friday

All About the Boy

Maths Series

Love Plus One

Also Available from NineStar Press

www.ninestarpress.com